TELL IT TO
THE HANGMAN

TELL IT TO
THE HANGMAN

•

James Rhodes

AVALON BOOKS
NEW YORK

5 5 3 8 2 3 2

To William G. Seif & Georgia Ray

He had drunk too much. He didn't really care. Now he had the money to do what he damned well pleased. For the first time; for the very first time in his life he didn't have to answer to anybody about his spending.

He didn't have to answer to the woman in the red and blue satin dress with the glittering, sparkling comb in her hair who sat with him and matched him drink for drink. When she had first sat down at the table, he had thought she looked used, puffy, and tough as year-old hardtack. But after a few belly warmers she seemed to shed the veneer of hardness and her features softened, even her voice was smooth as sorghum. She would never be considered beautiful, but she was a good listener.

"A whole satchel full," he said to her when she

asked him how much and where. "Right up those butt-wide stairs and in my room."

When she cocked her head to one side and then lowered her soot-black eyelids he pounded the table. "Ain't lyin'. You just wait here and I'll bring it down."

She still didn't look at him. He got to his feet and weaved across the floor that kept shifting under the soles of his boots. He grabbed the bannister to keep from falling. It was like climbing a steep, wavering mountain. By the time he got to the top he was breathing deep and heavy.

Down the hallway was his room, if he could just make it that far everything would be fine, just fine.

The walls on either side of him kept moving inward and outward and he had a hard time holding on until he reached the door to his room. Once inside he forgot why he was there, why he had made the trip.

He looked around with red-rimmed eyes as if he had never been there before. Then his gaze found the unmade bed and he staggered over and flopped down. He was asleep and snoring almost as soon as his head touched the bedspread.

The sounds from downstairs were muffled until the door opened quietly and someone stepped inside. The intruder paused for a few moments and then moved stealthily over to the bed and the sleeping man. The intruder listened and looked for any sign indicating that the man was not totally asleep. Assured in a few moments, the intruder picked up a pillow and with a quick, deadly thrust suffocated the sleeping man whose struggles were brief and merciful.

The intruder went about the room searching and collecting what had been intended. The door to the room opened and shut quietly letting the intruder out. The room was silent; the dead man stared upward at a crack in the ceiling with sightless eyes.

Chapter One

Lance Jordan tightened the slack on the reins and the bay gelding pranced and snorted to let the rider know that he understood what the signal meant. Ahead of him lay the Arizona town of Jubilee. Lance wondered if it would be like the other towns he had passed through in his search for Uncle Ephraim.

"Must you?" Susan Wells had asked, knowing it was a senseless question and, also, knowing in her heart, the answer.

"He's got to come back and face the people of this town," Lance had said.

"And you have to be the one to go."

"You know I do. It's just the way I am."

Susan's green eyes searched his face the way they always did, as though they could read his mind or as though they were trying to memorize his features.

4

"I know. Where do you think he went?"

"Arizona most likely. He always talked about going there."

Susan had fixed some food for him to take along. There was fried chicken, beans, salt pork, biscuit makings and a sack of ground coffee. She watched as Lance carefully arranged everything on the rear of the saddle. She always felt her heart was going out of her whenever Lance went away, even if it was just a day's journey to Las Palomas.

"Take me with you," Susan said urgently.

"I can't do that."

"Why not?"

"You know why not. Your papa would skin me from my nose to my toes if I done that."

Susan was aware of that, she only was making conversation so Lance would linger just a while longer. She and Lance had known they would wed some day ever since they were in the eighth grade. Lance had grown up on the Lazy B Ranch in San Anselmo which was about an hour ride from her father's spread.

"What about Boyd and the rest of your brothers? Why isn't one of them going along with you?"

"They got work to do at the ranch. I'm the only one free to go."

"Besides, you are the one who doesn't want to spend the rest of his life in San Anselmo."

Lance was finished packing. He was anxious to be on his way. The only thing he wasn't anxious to leave behind was Susan. Not that he didn't get along with his pa and ma and his brothers and sister, because he did. They were a warm, close family. It was just that Lance wanted to be on his own, to be his own man, to see if he could start from scratch like his pa had and make something of his life. In a way that was why he actually welcomed this trip, even though the reason he was going was not one he especially liked.

"Better be movin'," Lance said and before Susan could answer he planted a farewell kiss on her lips, then sprang into the saddle and rode away.

Lance glanced back one time and saw Susan waving to him. The sunlight glinted on her brown hair and she looked tiny and fragile standing there. Lance doffed his Stetson and waved back to her.

She'll be fine, he said to himself. Susan might seem fragile as a China doll, but she had grit in all her five-seven frame.

It wouldn't do to dwell on Susan, so Lance directed his attention to the trail ahead. The sun was beginning to slip toward the horizon when he made his first camp for the night.

Lance rubbed down his gelding and got a fire going with some sun-dried, gnarly wood he had gathered. He made some cowboy coffee, a fistful of grounds and a cup of water, and ate the fried chicken. He lay back on his saddle and looked up at the star-speckled sky not feeling alone but thinking about why he was on this mission.

Uncle Ephraim, always the rascal, was never to be trusted beyond his shadow. It wasn't a surprise that he had made off with the money—honest-given money from all the townsfolk in San Anselmo to help the Preeble family who had gotten burned out. Everything they owned in the world had gone up in flames when the cabin burned.

"We're oblidged as God-fearin' citizens to help them out," Uncle Ephraim, Lance's father's bachelor brother, had shouted at the town-council meeting.

Allowing Uncle Ephraim to hold the collection, it sounded like the right thing to do at the time, but it turned out to be the wrong thing to do. When a substantial amount had been collected, Uncle Ephraim and his high-spirited piebold disappeared from San Anselmo and New Mexico.

For two weeks Lance had ridden the trail from town to town. He got some encouragement along the way. Yep, there was a feller on a piebold through here not more'n a week ago. Headed? West, would be my guess.

So now Lance was ready to ride into Jubilee. He didn't think he would have any more luck here than anyplace else. All he knew for certain was he was getting low in supplies and he needed work if he was to continue his search.

"Let's move," Lance spurred his gelding into a fast trot for the remaining distance. When he got to the main street of the town, he slowed his pace to look around.

Jubilee was about five blocks long, as far as businesses went. There were some houses he could see away from the business district on the cross streets.

Lance went past a mercantile store with a hitching rail outside. Two wagons stood in front of the store and the teams were tethered to the hitching rail. An old, grey-haired thin-as-a-cactus-needle man came out of the store carrying a sack of grain over his sloping shoulders. The old man staggered under the weight and nearly fell. Lance was off his horse in a blink and rushed over to the old man.

"Here," Lance said, grabbing the sack of grain. "Let me do that."

The old man heaved a sigh of deep relief as Lance took the load from him.

"Thanks, young feller," the old man said. "Bit off more'n I could chew."

"Where do I put it?"

"Back of that wagon," the old man said, pointing to the nearest wagon.

Lance easily heaved the sack into the wagon next to the other stacked provisions.

A middle-aged woman wearing a cotton kerchief around her head came out of the store. "Put it all on our bill, Mr. Denker, please. My husband will make it good the end of the month."

She had seen what Lance had done and she thanked him before he helped her up on the driver's seat. "Right good to find somebody in these parts with nice upbringing. You got a fine helper here, Mr. Denker."

Before Lance could set her straight, the woman

snapped the reins and the team bolted down the street stirring up a cloud of thick, choking grey dust.

"That was Orie Tybolt's woman. She never hesitates to speak her mind—about anything. Didn't catch your handle?"

"Lance Jordan. Glad to be able to help."

The man Denker, Harley, as Lance later learned, pulled all of his skinny frame up to his full five-foot-five and said, "You new in Jubilee? Ain't seen you around before."

"Just passing through. Only I might be tempted to stay on."

"What might tempt you?"

"A job, a place to hang my saddle, and three squares," Lance replied and turned to leave.

"Hold on," Harley said. "If you work as good as you talk, I can use you here at my store. Lost my help two weeks ago. Off and went to Tucson. What say?"

Lance turned and looked at Harley and then the store. "I'd say you got yourself a hired hand. And I'm a worker, only. . . ."

Harley wobbled his head back and forth like a chicken looking for feed. "Only what?"

"I just want to look over the town for an hour or two. Try to find me a place to bed down while I'm here in Jubilee."

"Take your time. As for a place to bunk, I got a room off the store that's as good as any you'll find here in Jubilee. And it's cheap, rent free."

"Can't argue with that. I'll be back in an hour, Mr. Denker."

"Call me Harley. Just about everybody does, except them what owes me money."

Lance slipped into the saddle and headed downtown again. He passed Red Gulley, a bar that was full of raucous laughter and some drovers who were airin' their lungs even this early in the day.

Lance passed the saloon and looked at the eye-catching two-storied hotel built on the corner that looked down on Jubilee with snooty arrogance. Those weren't the words Lance would use to describe it, but they were those of Marshal Brad Crawley whose "hoosegow" was just across the street from The Pirate's Den.

Today Marshal Crawley was at his desk, his legs outstretched and his big, muscular arms folded behind his head. His attention was on the lone cowpuncher riding down the street. He was a stranger to Jubilee and as such Brad Crawley was always curious about any stranger who rode the streets of Jubilee.

Brad got to his feet, kicking the swivel chair away from the desk as he reached for his hat with the Montana peak. Marshal Crawley was a wide-shouldered, tall man with a slightly balding head, which he generally kept covered with his hat. He was clean shaven except for the bushy, hairy mustache that grew abundantly from beneath his wide, flat nose. He had broken his nose and gotten a game leg busting broncs in Wyoming when he was just fourteen.

Marshal Crawley walked outside and stood in the shade of the overhanging roof. He watched the lone rider as he approached and nodded when the man smiled at him and tipped the brim of his hat.

"Mornin' Marshal," the man said. "Name's Jordan. Lance Jordan. Got a nice friendly town here."

"Sometimes," Crawley said cryptically. "Passin' through?"

"Not for a while. Got me a job over at the mercantile store. Mr. Denker hired me just a while ago."

Brad Crawley listened and slowly nodded his head in understanding. Harley Denker was getting old, maybe too old to be tending the store. He should have sold out years ago and headed back East.

"Where you from?"

"New Mexico. A little town called San Anselmo. Ever hear of it?"

Brad Crawley didn't answer. If he didn't know of a place or of an event or anything from schoolbooks he wasn't interested. Crawley's world was of his own invention and he was the center of that world. He was its core and its universe. Brad Crawley was the sovereign Lord of his creation, and therefore invulnerable and impervious to death.

"Nice lookin' hotel over there," Lance went on, unoffended by the marshal's not answering his question.

"The Pirate's Den," Marshal Crawley said, and his mouth twisted into a smirk. "Right name for a den of thieves and outlaws."

Lance had turned to look at the hotel as the marshal

spoke. He thought you just couldn't judge a place from its outside. The hotel looked spankin' new and a worthy addition to any town.

"See you, Marshal," Lance said, and his gelding responded to his knees.

"Small town," Marshal Crawley said. "Sooner or later I have a run-in with everybody."

"I'll try to not have that happen," Lance said, and continued down the street. He could feel the marshal's rock-hard eyes on his back. Lance always wanted people to cotton to him, but every once in a while he ran into some contrary dog. Marshal Crawley ran with that pack. Lance doubted if the marshal liked anyone, 'cepting maybe himself.

Beyond the main street of Jubilee, Lance saw a Congregational church and a schoolhouse. They were both small and badly in need of upkeep and a good lick of paint.

Lance got off his horse and stood in front of the schoolhouse. From an open window he could hear the female voice of the schoolmarm explaining a history lesson to the children.

Lance tethered his horse to some shrubbery and walked over to the shade of an oak tree which stood at one side of the school. As he stood there the door to the school was flung open and a group of yelling, laughing children ran out.

Just as they had emerged, Lance's attention was drawn back to the main street. He heard the unmistakable sound of gunfire as the patrons of Red Gulley raced out of town in a drunken revel.

Lance saw that they would soon be passing the schoolhouse. Instinct took over and Lance's gun hand shot downward and came up with his Colt .45. Lance took a stance in front of the children who had crowded behind him.

The riders rode by, pretending they hadn't seen Lance with his weapon drawn.

"It's all right," Lance said, holstering the Colt. "They're gone."

"But they'll be back," the schoolmarm said from the edge of the children. She was middle-aged, plain-looking, and garbed in gingham, but she had a nice smile and pretty eyes. "Thanks for protecting the children."

Lance just returned the smile and touched the brim of his Stetson. "Those drovers come around all the time?"

"All the time," the schoolmarm replied. "They hang out either at the Red Gulley or at Captain Kidd's place."

"Captain Kidd?"

"His full name is Martin Kidd. Somewhere in his lifetime he acquired the captain. I don't know if he really is a captain or not, I seriously doubt it. He owns The Pirate's Den."

Lance put the name of the owner and the hotel to-gether. Now he knew why it was called The Pirate's

Den. The marshal, like the schoolmarm, wasn't all that impressed by the captain and his establishment.

"I don't believe we've met," the schoolmarm said. "I'm Harriett Abbott."

Lance gave his name. She extended her hand in greeting. It was rough and calloused, as though Harriett Abbott not only taught at the school but helped build it too.

"Are you new here to Jubilee?"

"Just today. Rode in from New Mexico. But it looks liked I'll be sticking around for awhile. Got a job at Mr. Denker's. He hired me today."

That seemed to please Harriett. She said as much and then got the children separated into groups as they waited for their pas and mas to come and pick them up.

For most of them, learning was something of a luxury. After the school hours they had chores to do in their homes. Then it was supper, cracking the books, and bedtime. Play was something that was done at recess or on Sunday afternoons after church.

"Mr. Denker could use some good help," Harriett said. "He's a hard worker, but I'm afraid he's getting a little too old to do any heavy lifting. I'm pleased he hired you, Mr. Jordan."

Harriett's husband came by then to pick her up. He took to Lance right away, as most people generally did. When Harriett told Tom Abbott that Lance stood up to the drunken drovers who fanned the sky with bullets, he said, "You must be pretty good with a gun. You aren't a 'leather slapper' are you?"

Lance quickly set Tom straight that he wasn't a gunslinger. "I just got in a lot of practice back home in San Anselmo. Me and my brothers would practice drawing and bottle thumping out on the range."

Before they departed in the wagon Tom was driving, he said, "Come over for supper some night, Mr. Jordan."

"I'd like that. Been a long time since I had anything for supper but biscuits and beans. And call me Lance."

"We'll stay in touch," Tom said, and Harriett nodded and smiled her thanks to Lance once again for what he had done earlier for the children.

Lance slipped into the saddle and headed toward the main street. He glanced back at the school and the church and then at the few houses that were scattered on the side streets. Lance decided quickly that he liked Jubilee. He wouldn't mind settling down here. He wondered if Susan would share his feelings.

The gelding set a gentle pace down the main street. Passing the marshal's office Lance didn't let his direct gaze falter in any way. He kept staring straight ahead, although he saw Brad Crawley out of the corner of his eye.

Lance wondered where the marshal was when the drovers had been splitting the air with their shooting. Maybe he had been down at the Red Gulley and hadn't been able to do much. Having sized the marshal up, Lance figured Brad Crawley was more fool than wiseman. He had known a few men in his life like the marshal. Men who wore their anger and bravado on their shoulders and each day sent out a dare to anyone unwise enough to challenge them.

Passing the marshal's office, Lance gazed at The Pirate's Den. He had only been in Jubilee a brief time and already he had heard nothing but bad words about it and the owner. Because of that Lance's curiosity was aroused. He wanted to know more about the tall, wide building. Lance knew that before he left Jubilee, he'd be inside that hotel, it was just something he knew deep down inside.

He moved on past the hotel and then urged his horse to pick up the pace because he'd promised Harley Denker he wouldn't be gone more than an hour.

Lance tethered his horse at the hitch rail and took off his hat to run his fingers through his shoulder-length dark hair. As he began to walk toward the store, a man came hurriedly out. He was about five-eleven, a skinny five-eleven, with a quick nervous action to his motions. He might have been good looking but his eyes were too close-set in his face, giving him the look of an ornery diamondback.

The man brushed Lance aside with a quick thrust of his arm and said, "Out of my way, drover. I got business to attend to."

Then the man slipped easily into the saddle of his roan stallion and spurred the animal into a gallop, kicking up a funnel of suffocating dust behind him.

Lance was still staring at the man as Harley Denker

came to the open door and said, "You just had your first run-in with the owner of The Pirate's Den."

Lance ran a hand across his forehead before saying, "So that's Captain Kidd, is it?"

Harley spit. "In the flesh, or so he's called. Let's get to work, son."

Chapter Two

Lance settled easily into life at Jubilee and working at Denker's Mercantile. He was a hard worker, a trait he acquired working on his pa's ranch back in San Anselmo, and he was healthy and didn't tire easily.

He not only carried merchandise around the store, he soon learned to take orders from behind the counter.

"He can't be real," Harley Denker said now and then to himself. "I gotta be the luckiest man in Arizona Territory."

But after a week went by, Harley relaxed knowing that Lance was here to stay and wouldn't be gallivanting over to Tucson or even further to California in the blink of an eye.

It didn't take long for the young girls in town to learn that a handsome, good-natured man was now working at Denker's. They found the flimsiest excuses to come into town, even if it was for a jar of evaporated vinegar.

Lance joshed with them and also had a special way of making each one of them feel very important. He never got serious about any one of them, his heart was still back in San Anselmo with Susan Wells. Now that he was working, he wrote her his first letter telling her all about Jubilee and how he still hadn't made any progress in locating the missing Uncle Ephraim.

Exactly one week to the day Lance started working at Denker's, he learned something about Uncle Ephraim. It was from a miner who had come in for supplies.

"Beans, coffee, sugar, dried potatoes," the miner counted off the supplies. "Match tins, bacon, rolled oats, plenty of salt and pepper. . . ."

The miner droned on as Lance checked the bagged supplies to make certain he hadn't shorted the grizzled, sun-baked, old geezer.

"You new here, reckon?"

"As such," Lance answered.

"You from?"

"New Mexico. Little town over there you never heard of."

"Try me. I ain't exactly the type who lets sand cake between his toes."

Lance told him where in New Mexico he hailed from. When he told him that he was from a ranch just north of San Anselmo, the miner put a thumb to his heavy growth of whiskers.

"San Anselmo. Seems I met a feller from there just the other day. Only the other day to me could mean a week or so ago. Lose track of time out there in the lonesome desert."

Lance was half listening to the old man, he wasn't sure what the miner was saying was exactly the gospel truth. But when he began to describe the man riding on the piebald, Lance gave him all his attention. The miner was describing Uncle Ephraim to a fare-thee-well.

"Did you catch the man's name?"

The miner scratched the bald spot on the crown of his head. "Let's see now. It's right there on the tip of my tongue. No, it's gone. Dammit! Gettin' old starts at the top and works down."

Lance was eager to find out if it was his uncle, but he didn't want to appear too eager. It might drive the name clean out of the miner's skull.

"Anything like Ephraim?" Lance asked.

The miner's cloudy eyes cleared up right away. "Ephraim! You betcha. That's it. Knew it had a bible ring to it. Ephraim was his name."

"Tell me about him. How long did you talk to him?" Lance leaned casually on the counter. He would get more out of the old miner if he played it loose.

"Not long. He was on his way here to Jubilee. Ridin' on that hellish piebold of his. Ornery horse, tried to give me a bite."

"So he's here in Jubilee."

"Said as much. Why all the interest in this Ephraim feller? You ask me, he's a man with a lot of trouble behind him."

Lance wanted to say more and learn more, but at that moment a customer entered the store.

"Need some help loading those supplies?" Lance asked.

The miner waved him off with a gnarled fist. "Been carin' for myself over sixty years now. Figure I can do the same until they throw those clods over my pine box."

After the miner left the store on bowed, awkward legs, Lance forgot about Uncle Ephraim as he turned his attention to the man who had come in for supplies. He was a short, stout, little man who worked for a rancher way out south of Jubilee. Benny was his name and Lance had met him at the saloon a few nights after he had arrived in Jubilee.

Benny wasn't the brightest man in the world and sometimes people took advantage of that. Benny didn't seem to mind, he was always cheerful and good-natured. Maybe that was why he took to Lance, since they both saw more sunshine than dark clouds in their daily lives.

"What can I do for you, Benny?" Lance asked, taking the hand-written list that the short man held up in his hand.

"Everything is on there, Lance. Just like they told me to write."

"You got good, clear handwriting, Benny," Lance said, and Benny beamed with pride.

Lance handed Benny a stick of horehound candy and then went about filling the order while Benny wandered around behind Lance watching his every move. While he was working, Tom Abbott came into Denker's.

"Just have to pick up a few things, Lance," Tom said affably.

"Hi there, Benny, you been working real hard for Ben Taggart?"

Benny bit off a chunk of the horehound. "Try to. Mr. Taggart, he's a real nice man. He takes good care of them who work for him."

Tom agreed that Benny was right. "But you are a good worker too, Benny. You are real good with your hands. Real good."

Like Lance, Tom Abbott was considerate of Benny. Maybe because there were always so many school kids hanging around the house. He just naturally placed Benny in the category of a child.

Tom didn't linger, he found what he needed, paid for it, and left the store.

Harley wandered in while Lance was finishing up Benny's order.

"Howdy, Benny. Tell Ben Taggart I said the same to him. Tell him, also, I got that order in for him with that company in Chicago. Will you do that?"

Benny said he would. Lance put the last of Benny's

order on the counter and made out a bill which he put on the spindle that would be paid faithfully the last of the month.

"Need any help, Benny?" Lance asked, stuffing the last item in the box.

"Naw, I can carry this. Mr. Taggart's wagon is down at the farrier's. He's talkin' to Abel Kinkaid."

"I'll load you up. Least I can do," Lance said. Benny allowed him this latitude. Then he shoved the last piece of the horehound into his mouth and walked with slow, deliberate steps out the door.

Lance and Harley watched Benny leave and they also saw a heavy-set man with a pock-marked face put a hand on Benny's shoulder.

Lance didn't like the man from the git go. He never tried to judge a man by his looks, but this drover was mean ugly.

"Who's that?" Lance asked, keeping a wary eye on Benny.

"Wade Briley. Goes by the name of Hap. Runs with the gang that hangs out at The Pirate's Den. He's trouble on spurs. Always drinkin' and trying to better anyone at the draw."

Lance saw that Benny was trying to get free from the tight grip Hap Briley had on him. He was squirming and doing his best to get away. It was something that Lance couldn't stand still for.

"Be right back," Lance said, and Harley knew right away where he was headed and the reason.

Lance stepped outside just as Hap Briley took the

hunk of horehound out of Benny's mouth and ground it under the heel of his boot.

"Let him go," Lance said, and Hap's twisted smile turned into an angry smirk.

"Who's gonna make me? You?"

"That's right."

Hap ignored Lance and went back to tormenting Benny who was still trying to inch away.

"I said, let him go," Lance repeated, then with a lightning swift thrust of his fist in a jarring uppercut sent Hap sprawling on the boardwalk.

Hap's chin spurted a jagged line of red and spittle oozed down from the side of his mouth. His hand reached for his gun but Lance stomped on it and Hap let out an anguished wail. Lance bent over and quickly relieved Hap of his revolver.

"You get this back when you make it up to Benny," Lance said.

But Benny was shaking so hard he almost dropped the box of supplies. "It's all right, Lance. It's all right. He didn't mean no harm."

He did mean harm, Lance thought, *but Benny was afraid of his hog on man's legs.* That's what he smelled like to Lance, a lazy, wallowing hog that spent his life eating rotten food.

Hap wiped the blood from his chin with the sleeve of his shirt. He staggered to his feet and stood in a hunched position ready to charge Lance if he made a mistaken move.

"Gimme my gun!" he said spitting some blood from his mouth.

"Give it back, Lance," Benny pleaded. "I don't want no trouble."

Lance had been around polecat bullies like Hap Briley before. You had to face up to them; once they got the upper hand, once they felt they had you cowed, there was no stopping their tormenting.

But Benny couldn't reason this out. All he wanted was to be away from Hap Briley and back with Mr. Taggart where it was safe, where he could clean out the corral and be around the horses who never said anything, no questions asked, no answers expected.

Lance could read this in Benny's actions. He felt Benny had to face enough difficult things during the day and he didn't want to add to his burden. Opening the gun he emptied the bullets from the chamber. Then he handed the revolver back to Hap Briley.

Before Briley left, he said, "Bullets are easy to come by. You just better watch yourself, dung face. I'll be watchin' for you."

Lance had been threatened before in his lifetime, by better men than Wade Briley.

"It's a two-way street," Lance said, as Hap holstered his revolver. "And Jubilee's a small town."

Hap walked away in the direction of The Pirate's Den. He glanced back once at Lance and Benny. Lance wasn't sorry he had come to Benny's assistance. He was only sorry that it might cause the gentle little man grief down the line from that hog of a man.

"Thanks, Lance," Benny said looking sorrowfully at the smashed remains of the horehound. "I gotta get over to the farrier's."

"Wait up," Lance said, and he hurried back inside the store. He came back with another horehound stick and Benny's face lit up. With his simple mind he had thankfully forgotten all about his encounter with Hap Briley now that this unexpected bounty had been bestowed upon him.

"Gosh, thanks, Lance," Benny said, and he hurried down the street toward the farrier's.

"Not the smartest thing in the world you just did," Harley said when Lance returned to work.

"You mean giving Benny some more horehound?"

"I mean tangling with Hap Briley. He's walkin' trouble. Don't matter to Hap what he does to a feller. Or how he does it for that matter."

Lance just shrugged. He hoisted a flour sack onto the counter.

"I'll take my chances."

Harley moved a canister with the toe of his boot. "Just warnin' you. Good help ain't easy to come by these days."

Lance chuckled and Harley acted as though he really had meant what he said. He decided to change the subject. "What do you know about Marshal Crawley?"

"What you askin'?"

"Just wondering. Met him the first day I came to

Jubilee. Kinda curious about the man. Been marshalin' long?"

Harley sat down on a pickle barrel. "Got to rest this game shoulder of mine for a minute. You was askin' about Marshal Crawley? Not much to tell. Came from Wyoming. That's where he got that limp of his. Some bronc sent him to get a skyfull. Brad's been here about a year now. We all voted him into office, seein's how there weren't any other candidates."

Lance knew from the little time he had been with Harley Dinker that that was about all he would get out of him concerning Marshal Crawley. Instead, Harley went back to talking about Hap Briley.

"He's been hanging out over at The Pirate's Den more and more lately. Heard tell he's the head honcho for Captain Kidd's outfit."

"Got to go into that place one of these days and see it for myself. Heard a lot of tales about it ever since I came to Jubilee," Lance said.

"Wouldn't, unless it was an absolute necessity."

"Why not?"

"Too many men turn up fodder for Boot Hill over there."

Lance was more than curious about that.

"What are you talking about, Harley? Something going on over there that ain't lawful?"

Harley shifted his skinny frame on the barrel.

"All I know is that a lot of drovers and strangers passing through Jubilee never make it out of town once they stop at that place."

"You aren't joshin'?"

"Not a pip. Go check the cemetery, lot of plain wooden headboards out there with just a name scratched on them."

"Somebody is killing people over there? Why isn't Marshal Crawley doing something about it?"

Harley reached out and straightened a container of jerky that was catawampus on the counter. "What can you do if it's all legal like?"

Lance leaned over the counter. He kept trying to look Harley squarely in the eye, but the rail-thin man kept avoiding eye contact. "What do you mean it's all legal?"

"When you got the town coroner in your pocket, you can do pretty durn what you feel like."

"Who's the town coroner? And what's he got to do with anything?"

"That's right. You ain't met Saw Hogan yet. He's the local coroner, or mortician, if you want to get fancy. He and Martin Kidd are close as tics in a mattress. Don't know what Kidd's got on Hogan, but it must be something."

Lance waited patiently. He knew that sometimes Harley took a long way around the loop before he got to the point.

"Hogan hangs out at the Den. Any hour of the day you can find him at the bar. Likes his Barleycorn and lots of it. He's an odd duffer. Friendly as all git out when he's got a gut burner in him. He can quote one of them fancy poets word for word. When he's sober, he's a changed man. Can't get more'n a dozen words out of him."

That was it for the time being. Some ranchers wandered in and Lance went to work. Even as he filled the orders he kept mulling over what Harley had said, but more importantly, what the miner had said about Uncle Ephraim.

The following day, Harley closed up the store to drive to Tucson.

"Take some time to yourself, young feller," Harley said as he climbed aboard his wagon. Harley had never married, so there was only Lance to see him off. Harley was beginning to feel somewhat paternal toward Lance, who could have been the son he never had. "Ride out and see the country. You been workin' real hard."

"I'll do that," Lance said. "Watch yourself over in Tucson. Lots of pretty gals over there."

Harley just shook his head. "At my age, I just look."

With that Harley snapped the reins and rode down the dusty street headed for the outskirts of Jubilee. Lance watched him until he made the turn leaving Main Street behind him.

Now that Harley was gone, Lance saddled up his gelding and headed north of town. He could see for miles across the flat, level land. Above him the golden-bronze sun rode in a cloudless blue sky. There was a faint breeze that made the ride as enjoyable as Lance had expected.

Only Lance really was not all that interested in neck

craning. He kept thinking about the miner who had come into Denker's and had told him about the stranger he had seen riding the piebold. It couldn't have been anyone else but Uncle Ephraim, Lance was positive of that.

He was also thinking about Susan and how much he longed for her. Now he looked for the first time at the land. This was where he wanted to settle down. This was where he might sink roots. But that would come after he completed his mission and found Ephraim Jordan and the absconded money. That would be after he turned Uncle Ephraim over to the hands of the San Anselmo law and the money to the deserving people.

All of that was down the line. He would have plenty of time to think about that later. Lance spurred the gelding and galloped across the open range.

It was late afternoon when Lance rode back into Jubilee. He was hot, dusty, and hungry as a winter-starved grizzly. He tethered his horse outside the store and went inside to the back where his room was located. It was spare and small, but Lance didn't need much more than that.

He tore off his shirt and filled the basin with water from the porcelain pitcher. Lance splashed his face with water and towelled down. He ran a comb through his long, dark-brown hair which was slightly damp and curling at the tips.

Lance put on a clean pull-over work shirt with a mule-eared collar, tucking it in. He grabbed a soiled piece of cotton fabric and brushed his fifteen-dollar tailor-made boots to a fine shine.

He was ready to go into town and have his supper. Outside, he led his horse to the small corral behind the store and rubbed the animal down, something he had almost forgotten to do. Then Lance strode across the boardwalks headed toward the Red Gulley.

At this time of the day, just at sundown, the part-saloon, part-eatery was quiet. The place smelled heavily of stale cigarette smoke and cheap rotgut. But the brass overhead lamps were clean and the mirror behind the bar was spotless.

There was one man leaning against the bar and Lance ordered a beer from the bartender and steak and potatoes.

"Take a seat, Stranger," the barkeep said. "Callie May will bring your vittles over."

"Stranger, huh!" The beefy, florid-faced man with the scraggly, thin-wisps of hair looked at Lance. " 'Stranger! Behold, interred together, The souls of learning and of leather.' " He belched and made an effusive apology.

"What's the name, Stranger? I'm called Saw Hogan."

Lance immediately recognized the coroner from Harley Denker's description.

"Lance Jordan. I'm working at Denker's Mercantile."

Saw Hogan took a quick swallow from his glass of

whiskey. "Good man, that Harley Denker. I might even say a veritable prince among men."

Lance wouldn't have gone that far, but he didn't protest. He could see that Saw Hogan was pretty far along the way to getting well preserved for the night.

"I've heard of you," Lance said. "You're the local undertaker."

Saw Hogan reached for his glass of whiskey with a faintly trembling hand. "Sad but true. I do my work, the best way I can. You may not believe this, but at one time I was one of the ten best morticians in New York State."

Lance settled in a chair and Hogan followed him over to the table. "Have a seat and tell me about it," Lance offered his friendship.

"I'll stand," Hogan said. "That way I can keep the room from spinning and causing bodily harm to any innocent bystander."

Lance was amazed that as drunk as Saw Hogan must have been, you couldn't tell it from his speech which was smooth and unslurred.

"Wait for just a moment," Hogan said as he went back to the bar for a refill on his drink. He came back on slightly unsteady legs. Taking a deep draw on the sour mash, he wiped his lips with a kerchief and let out a deep sigh of pleasure. "Brew of the gods!"

Lance took a sip of his beer and put the mug down as he waited for Saw Hogan to speak again.

"Told you I was from New York, didn't I? Great little city. I had quite a practice going there. Things happen in life and the first thing you know you find yourself out in the wilds of Arizona."

This burst of rhetoric caused Hogan to take a deep swallow from his glass. He put one hand on the back of a chair to steady himself.

"Business must be pretty good in Jubilee," Lance said. "Otherwise you would be moving on."

Saw Hogan was feeling garrulous and this stranger was a likable sort. You couldn't really call him a stranger since he was now gainfully employed by Harley Denker. But Hogan never went beyond the point in his drinking where he wasn't in control of what he was saying.

"Business is good."

"Lots of drovers and drunken cowboys?"

"Them and others."

"You are the last person who sees them."

Hogan gulped down another swig of the Barleycorn. "An old joke goes that an undertaker is your best friend. He's the last person to let you down."

Lance didn't much care for graveyard humor, but he did manage a slight smile for Hogan's benefit. "You know much about The Pirate's Den? Hear tell it's quite a place."

"That it is. I get a lot of business from Captain Kidd's establishment."

"You know this Captain Kidd?"

"Pretty well. You sure are one for asking questions."

Lance put a hand on his mug of beer. "Just trying

to be friendly. New in town, want to learn as much as I can about Jubilee."

"I'd be careful about asking too many questions, Jordan. Not in this town, anyway. Could get you into deep trouble. Understand?"

Lance said that he did. Before Hogan could say anything else, Callie May came to the table. She was a buxom girl with bad teeth who could out-cuss any drover and did the cooking and table waiting.

"You ought to have something in that gut of yours besides hooch, Hogan," Callie May said. "Let me fetch you a steak and some johnny cakes."

Saw Hogan turned visibly pale at the suggestion. "Callie May, my sweet dove. You are a treasure. 'A violet by a mossy stone, half hidden from the eye! Fair as a star, when only one is shining in the sky.' But no thanks. I bid you both good night."

Callie May shrugged as Saw Hogan weaved his way to the batwing doors. The waitress hurried back to the kitchen while Lance ate his supper. He had made up his mind on the way from San Anselmo that he wouldn't tell anyone about the money Uncle Ephraim had made off with. You just never knew about people. Lance felt he was getting close to finding out something about Uncle Ephraim. Maybe Jubilee held the answer.

Lance ate, finished his beer, and paid the barkeep. Then he strode outside feeling satisfied and slightly stuffed from Callie May's cooking.

There was a full moon tonight and because of that, Lance saw the wink of light reflected off the gun barrel across the street. At that moment, there was a bright flash as the gun was fired directly at him.

Chapter Three

At the first flick of the moonlight on the six-shooter, Lance hit the boardwalk. The bullet pinged against the front of the Red Gulley and whined into the night.

Lance reached for his Colt .45 and had it aimed across the street as he lay in a prone position. He could see easily by the bright light of the moon. But whoever had taken a pot shot at him was gone. The only sound he heard was the sighing of the wind down from the North.

After a few minutes, Lance got himself into a crouching position. Even though the shooter was not visible, he didn't want to take a chance and make himself an easy target.

He was tempted to go down the street to the marshal's office and tell Crawley what had happened. Lance decided against that plan of action. He just wasn't all that confident that Marshal Crawley would believe him. Hearing one single gunshot in Jubilee at night apparently was an old story to the marshal.

Lance remained in the crouched position for a few minutes until he was certain he was out of danger. Then he stretched himself to his full six-foot-four. Slowly and cautiously as a wary mountain cat, he moved down Main Street toward the store.

The only person who had anything against him in Jubilee was Hap Briley. He had been expecting something like this ever since he had come to Benny's defense. Lance hadn't expected a bushwhacker, but now he knew the sort of yellow dog he was dealing with.

He stayed in the shadows as much as he could, daring only to come out into the bright moonlight when he neared the store.

Lance was glancing to the right across the street and occasionally to his back. It would just be the sort of thing a polecat like Briley would be adept at, back-shooting. As he came up to the store, he saw a worn-out chestnut stallion near the front door.

"Store's closed for the day," Lance said as he approached the man who stepped out from the shadows. He was a gaunt, hollow-cheeked man with piercing, sunken green eyes.

"Harley'll let me in," the man said. "He and me's been friends a long time. You his new hand?"

Lance said he was. "Name's Jordan, Lance Jordan."

"Pleased to meet up with you, Jordan. You can call me Reuben Mundy."

They shook hands. Up close, Lance saw the tattered, grease-stained work shirt, the Levi's that were patched at the knees, and the boots that were run over at the heels. Reuben Mundy wasn't exactly the most prosperous rancher that traded at Harley's.

"Harley's over at Tucson. He'll be back in the morning," Lance was quick to inform Reuben.

"All I need is some beans for supper. The kids are gettin' hungry and my old lady's stowed up with her bad back."

Lance had heard Harley talk about Reuben Mundy and his family. How they once had a good-size spread south of town by the Mesquite River. Somehow Reuben had lost it all. Harley had been vague about the conditions. Now the Mundys lived in a small shack and he did odd jobs around town to make ends at least try to meet. Harley had a tab he wrote for Reuben in front of him which he tore up the moment the man had left the store.

"Come on," Lance said, knowing that this was what Harley would have done himself.

They went inside the store and Lance dealt out some beans for Mundy who also managed to talk him out of some salt pork and some licorice for the kids.

"Would you put it on my bill?" Reuben said. "I'll be in Friday to make it good."

"I'll do that," Lance said and wrote something on a a slip of paper not desiring to take anything away from Reuben Mundy's dignity as a man and breadwinner.

Mundy thanked Lance and started to move away.

Then he stopped and turned back. "You have some kinda run-in with Hap Briley? Reason I'm askin' is that I saw him across from the Red Gulley tonight with his six-gun pulled out."

"He was giving Benny some sorrow the other day. Benny don't bother anyone and I don't tolerate anyone bothering him."

"So that's it. I saw Briley take a shot at you. Wondered what you'd done."

"Are you sure it was Hap Briley?"

Mundy's mouth twisted like a baited worm. "Couldn't been mistaken. I'd know that rotten lowlife anywhere. If I didn't see him, I could always smell him."

Lance opened the door for Mundy who once again thanked Lance and then said, "You know, I didn't always look this way. I used to wear pretty fancy suits on Saturday nights and I provided for my family. I once had a pair of fifty-dollar boots. Sharp as a honed razor I was. Then I lost it all. All to that bastard Kidd over at The Pirate's Den. He cheated at cards. Got my savings, my spread, and my pride."

Lance listened carefully. He had no real sympathy for anyone who was foolish enough to gamble. Especially if he had a wife and young 'uns to look after.

"Some day Kidd will get his. You just wait and see. Hope I'm around when it happens."

Lance closed the door after Reuben had gone and stood there for a moment thinking about what he had said in regards to Hap Briley. It was just as Lance had figured. Briley was getting back at him for the beating he had took in front of the store. Too bad for Briley that he was such a bad shot.

From the shadows of the overhanging wooden shelter at the jail, Marshal Crawley had heard the single shot that Hap Briley had fired at Lance. In Jubilee one bullet spent was no cause for any great alarm. Those drunken cowpokes a week or so ago who poked holes in the sky with their six-shooters, that was when you got a little edgy. Even then, as Brad Crawley had learned the hard way, you didn't get too edgy because they would soon be riding out of town.

Crawley lit a cigarette he had rolled and let the smoke ease in lazy tendrils from his nostrils. He was thinking tonight about his wife Laura Anne, dead almost five years now. She had been taking care of a neighboring family down with small pox and ended up being the one who died from the disease.

He ran a hand over his slightly balding head that was fringed with straw-colored hair. Ever since Lura Anne had gone, he didn't give a hoot in Hades about his appearance. He didn't even care if people stared at his limp-walk from that fall he had taken busting a mean-as-a-turpentined-dog back in Cheyenne.

These days Crawley was just biding his time as a marshal. He knew that his big-shouldered six-foot frame intimidated most drovers and he hadn't been challenged to a draw. Crawley was a fair gunman, but he imagined himself better than he actually was. Crawley was a braggart at heart, and his feelings, along with his emotions, had been buried with his wife on a wind-whipped hill in Wyoming.

Crawley stepped out of the shadows in order to get a better look at the clientele who was coming and going from the Pirate's Den. Crawley had no love for Captain Martin Kidd or any of the gang who kowtowed to his every whim. He knew that the men who rode with Hap Briley were lawless, but he didn't want to make any ripples in the pond. Besides, he was just one man against a small army. What did Jubilee expect from him? Best to just look the other way sometimes.

The lights in the Cutlass Room were turned low. There was a fiddler on the stage who was playing, "Mother, Kiss Me In My Dreams," to a half-empty room. At a corner table, Martin Kidd, better known as Captain, was slowly shuffling a deck of cards as he listened to Wade Briley talk between slurps of rotgut.

"I almost pegged him," Briley chuckled. "He was just comin' out of Red Gulley. But I missed him by that much. Damn worst shot I ever fired."

Kidd continued to shuffle the cards. He was a medium-sized man with a lean, wiry body. Martin Kidd was not particularly good-looking mainly because his eyes were too narrowly set in his face, giving him the look of a predatory animal.

He had come by the name Captain when he and a band of roughnecks had raided mining camps in the Yukon. Kidd was a natural-born leader; when it came to any criminal activity, that is. Even in school he had been the one behind the mischief and broken bones that happened with regularity when he was around. Not only was Kidd involved in mischief, he also had a hand in gambling and wasn't above cheating on any test or exam that came along.

Kidd was born a disobedient and willful person. He had hated authority since childhood. When he was twelve, he threatened his father with a gun. By the time he had finished schooling he was well on his way to a life of criminal pursuits.

That pursuit took him to Alaska and the gold fields. Martin Kidd was too much of a miscreant to dig or pan for the gold. It didn't take him long to gather a gang of men who weren't too particular as to how they made their day's wages.

Here in this land of extremes he acquired the name Captain. More because of his last name than any other reason. During one of the more lucrative raids, a posse of local townspeople ambushed them as they were making away with the gold.

The surprise, violent confrontation left nearly all of his band either dead or fatally wounded. Martin was the only one who escaped unharmed and with all the gold intact. Seeing that Alaska was not the place for him any longer, he headed south to the States. Martin Kidd ended up finding the perfect place for himself and his style of living. Jubilee was a small town that needed a good hotel for the passengers staying overnight from the stage and the drovers and miners who wandered into town looking for a little fun and a nice soft bed to sleep in.

Martin did not lack for funds and The Pirate's Den came into being and was the talk of several towns in that part of Arizona. Once the hotel was built, it wasn't long before men like Hap Briley came along in need of someone to give them orders and provide for their comforts with aged whiskey and ladies of easy virtues.

It wasn't long before the women found out that Captain Martin Kidd was a tough taskmaster with a mean streak that left several of them needing help from Saw Hogan if they ran afoul of him and his temper. The only one who seemed to get along with Kidd was Rose Sparks who hailed from a small town in Nebraska. So far in their relationship, Martin had been tolerant in his dealings with her. Dealings that included an intimacy Kidd rarely shared with any of the other ladies.

Still shuffling the cards, Kidd listened while Hap Briley spoke of his intentions toward that mule turd working over at the mercantile store.

"I don't want you to try that again," Kidd said, momentarily ceasing the shuffling of the cards. "At least, not here in Jubilee. Outside of town, I could be less interested."

Hap mumbled something about how he aimed to get rid of Lance Jordan, but he wouldn't dare cross Captain Kidd, at least not to his face. "If you say as much. Anyway, I'm out to get that drover. Can you believe him standing up for that dummy?"

Kidd just shrugged. He didn't feel one way or the other about crazy Benny. At the moment he didn't want any undue attention drawn to The Pirate's Den.

"You didn't get any grief from Marshal Crawley?"

Hap took a swift swallow of his whiskey and wiped the dribble from his chin with his shirt sleeve. "He knows better than that. Crawley doesn't poke his head out of that jailhouse unless it's to have a smoke or get some grub from the boarding house."

"Don't write him off. He might surprise you someday," Kidd said, starting the shuffle again. "Haven't made up my mind about the marshal yet."

The fiddler had finished his song and now was playing a sweet version of "Beautiful Dreamer."

"You got any use for that piebold?" Hap asked in a casual, off-handed way. "I've taken a liking to him."

Again Kidd lifted his shoulders in a shrug. "Let it lay low for a while. Hogan just signed the death certificate a few days ago. You did bury him good?"

"Six feet under. Just like the others. Ain't going to do no more loud-mouthin' like he did that last night with Rose."

At the mention of her name, Rose got up from a table near the mahogany bar and walked over to where they were seated.

"Get lost," Kidd said to Hap who got to his feet whenever the Captain spoke in that tone of voice. "Sit down, Rose. It's been a while since we talked."

Hap made an awkward, stumbling exit from the table to the bar where he ordered another whiskey. Under his breath, the barkeep heard him say something that sounded like, "Someday I'll be head honcho around here and I won't have to take no orders from some fancy talker like him."

The barkeep didn't pay Hap any mind since he was noted for bragging with very little to brag about.

At the table, Rose sat down opposite Martin. She had come a long way from Broken Bow, Nebraska. And she had met a lot of men along the way. They were easy to figure out. But when it came to Captain Martin Kidd, she had no ready answers for how he thought or the way he behaved.

"Slow night," Rose said, touching the glitter-comb that protruded out from her pile of reddish hair.

"It'll pick up," Kidd said. "There was a herd boss in here a while ago. He said some of his men would be headed for Jubilee tonight."

Rose leaned forward. "That last man, the one from out of town, the one who kept boasting about his money. Whatever happened to him?"

Kidd reached over and grabbed hold of Rose's left wrist. He squeezed it so hard tears welled up in Rose's eyes.

"You just do your job, understand? Don't ask too many questions. You could get into a barrel of trouble that way."

Rose wanted to tell Kidd that he was hurting her, but she knew from past experiences that he would only tighten his grip on her wrist.

"Just askin', Cap," Rose said. "You know I always do what you tell me."

Slowly, as a smile spread across his face, Kidd released his hold on Rose. He looked at her in the dim light cast from the wall lamp. Her best feature was her fire-colored hair. She was mildly pretty, with a good figure that hadn't been too damaged by the life she lived.

Without another word, Kidd got to his feet and swept Rose into his arms as he waltzed her across the smooth, wooden floor. He had managed to learn his manners and his ersatz civility in his youth. Somewhere along the pathway of life he had acquired the bearing of a gentleman, which surfaced from time to time in unexpected ways.

Rose did her best to follow the Captain's swift footwork, not daring to miss a step or falter in any way. She was not a particularly good dancer, but she did her best to make the waltz seem as effortless as possible.

The fiddler kept on playing the waltz, also mindful of his employer's quick mood changes. He knew from past experiences that he would continue with a song that drew favor from Captain Kidd until he was told to cease by a curt nod from the owner of The Pirate's Den.

Rose was thankful when the Captain had had his fill of dancing and the music stopped.

"You aren't the worst dance partner I've ever had," Kidd said to Rose's surprise. "But you aren't the best either. Get back to your table, I got work that needs my attention."

Somewhat relieved that the waltz was ended and Kidd hadn't humiliated her as he had so often done in the past, Rose walked away. Not to her table but to the music stand.

The fiddler was checking some of the strings on his bow. When he saw Rose, he smiled. "Look real pretty tonight, Rose."

"Thanks, Tully," Rose said. "You always make me feel good."

"And you danced good too. Only . . ."

"Only what?"

"Why do you let him treat you the way he does?"

Rose shrugged. "Why do you?"

Tully didn't answer.

"Someday he'll get his," Rose said, off-handedly. "Someday you can count on it. How about something with a little pepper in it, Tully? Just for old Rose."

Tully raised his hand with the bow to the fiddle and began to play, "Dance My Lady Round and Round." Rose clapped her hands in time to the music and slowly turned to see Captain Kidd leave the Cutlass Room and head toward his office. Then she stomped her feet and egged Tully on to a faster beat.

It was around noon when Harley returned from Tucson. Lance had opened the store and met his boss as he stepped down from the wagon.

"Good to be back," Harley said.

"Have a good trip?"

"Always do. Tucson is a friendly place. But it's always right fine to be back. How you doin'?"

"Fine, just fine. Had a few customers while you were gone."

Harley took a few minutes to listen to Lance. He had missed the young man and had taken a real liking to him. He had been thinking all the way back from Tucson just how lucky he was to have had Lance come along when he did.

Lance decided not to say anything about Hap Briley taking a pot shot at him. No need to worry the old man unnecessarily. Instead, Lance told him about taking a ride to see the countryside.

"So you like it around here, do you?"

"Wouldn't mind settling down in Jubilee. That is, if Susan takes a liking to it."

"You're really taken by that girl, ain't you."

Lance just beamed. There was no need for him to answer that question. Harley could tell by Lance's actions and the way he spoke about the female back in New Mexico that Lance was smitten.

"Give me a hand unloadin', will ya?"

Lance got to work. He handed Harley all the lightweight boxes and carried the heavier ones himself into the store. He mentioned, while they worked, about Reuben Mundy coming in.

"Didn't charge him, did ya?"

Lance shook his head. "Like you do. I made some

scratch marks on a piece of paper. When Mundy left I tossed it away."

Surprisingly, that brought a chuckle from Harley. "Can't help it if we fall on hard times every once in a while. Even sometimes when we bring it on ourselves. Feller needs a little boostin' help now and again."

As Lance unloaded the last package, Harley said to him, "That goes to Captain Kidd over at The Den. You wanna take it over? Sort of special delivery."

"Be glad to. Been wanting to have a looksee at that place. Everyone I talk to in town tells me about the place. I should see for myself what all the talk's about."

"You do that. It's quite an establishment. Too bad it ain't under different management."

"No love lost between you and Captain Kidd."

"How can you lose a love you never had in the first place?" Harley said but with a touch of humor in his eyes. "You go on. I can handle the unwrappin' of these boxes."

"I'm on my way," Lance said, shouldering the carton that was to be delivered to Martin Kidd.

Lance's step was brisk as he strode along the boardwalk. He was anxious to get a good look at the place. He was also anxious to get a second look at Captain Kidd. The first encounter was rude and crude and he just wanted to see how Kidd behaved in his own environment.

He pushed through the door leading into the plush

lobby and came to an abrupt stop as he took in the deep, thick carpet and the paneled walls. There were chandeliers hanging from the ceiling, throwing just enough light on the lobby to give it a kind of unreal quality.

Lance walked over to the long counter where a clerk was busy writing something in a ledger.

"Package for Martin Kidd," Lance said and the man glanced up at him. "It came in today from Tucson."

"The Captain's in the Cutlass Room," the clerk said in a friendly voice. "That's right over there through those doors."

"Obliged," Lance said, as he lifted the package from the counter and headed in the direction the clerk had pointed.

Lance opened the batwinged doors and went into the bar. He stood there for a moment and then the first person he saw staring at him with hate-filled eyes was Hap Briley.

Chapter Four

For an instant, the two men stared at each other. Lance was alert and ready for any action. Hap Briley tried to stare Lance down, but he blinked and his hand did not move toward his six-shooter because he had caught the reflection of Captain Kidd in the mirror behind the bar.

The barkeep, ever attuned to any trouble that might be brewing, walked down to the end of the bar near to where Lance was standing. "What's your pleasure, Stranger?"

Lance's eyes slowly shifted from Hap Briley to the squat bartender with the dark, needle-tipped mustache. "Got something here for Martin Kidd. Been told I could find him in here."

The barkeep glanced at a table near the window. He

nodded in that direction. "You'll find him over at that table."

"Thanks."

As Lance passed Hap Briley, the outlaw turned his head to deliberately avoid Jordan.

Lance paused beside Briley. "You doin' much target practice these nights?"

Briley couldn't ignore Lance, but he remembered what Captain Kidd had told him.

"A little. Only I don't see as how that's any of your business."

"Wouldn't be if I didn't figure I might be a moving target."

Briley took one quick look at Martin Kidd, gulped down his whiskey and started to leave. Before he went too far, he turned to Lance and said, "Any time you feel like gettin' in some real target practice I'll meet you outside of town."

"I'm always available," Lance said, as Hap's shoulder muscles tightened when he left the room.

Lance looked over at the table where Captain Kidd was seated. He was all alone, but you got the impression a million eyes were watching his every move.

The owner of The Pirate's Den looked up from the cards he had dealt himself and his practiced eyes sized up Lance. He might make a good gunslinger, Kidd thought. Might be worth watching. He could always use a man fast with a gun. He nodded to Lance who came over to the table with the package.

"You must be Martin Kidd," Lance said. "If you

are, I got a package for you. Something you ordered from Tucson."

"So you're Harley Denker's new hired hand. Been hearing a lot about you lately. Care for a drink?"

Lance shook his head. "No, thanks. I just came to drop this off. That and see what The Pirate's Den looks like."

Kidd moved the box around on the table. "So what do you think?"

"I'm impressed."

"I spared no expense. It's the best hotel in the whole state. I guarantee that."

Lance wouldn't have gone that far, but he reserved judgment.

"You must be Lance Jordan, am I right?"

"On the money. I only got in town a while back. Seems a lot of folks around here know me."

"It's a small town."

"And could be a nice town."

"Could be?"

Lance was sizing Martin Kidd up too. He saw a medium-sized man with a lean, lithe body. His face was smooth-shaven and the black, bushy eyebrows hovered over his narrow-set eyes. Maybe it was just the light in the place, but Lance could swear as he talked to the man he never once blinked.

"Jubilee is like any new town, got to shake itself of any bad company. Once that gets taken care of, then the place has a chance to grow."

Martin Kidd's eyebrows rose slightly as Lance

spoke. He had been wrong about the man, he wouldn't make a good gun fanner, he was too full of goody-goody ideas. Maybe he should have let Briley take care of him, anywhere and anytime. Kidd put the cards down and stood up, taking the package in his hands.

"If you won't have a drink, then I have work to do in my office. Take a look around before you leave, Mr. Jordan."

"I'll do that. Been a pleasure meeting you."

Kidd wasn't certain that was true, yet he nodded as he walked away from the table.

Lance watched the owner of The Den leave the room. As he was turning to leave, a woman came over to the table. She was wearing a gaudy-colored dress and she was smoking a cheroot. The most outstanding thing about her was her red hair and the glittering comb that topped it.

"Never seen you in here before," the woman said in a honeyed voice. "Name's Rose."

Lance gave Rose his first name.

"You ain't the new man over at Denker's, are you?"

"That's right. Harley took me on just a couple of weeks ago."

Rose looked at Lance closely by the light of the lamp. She reached up and touched his face, moving it so that she could get a better look at it.

"Funny. Got the feelin' I either seen you before or you look familiar to me. Ever been here before?"

"First time. Quite a place."

Rose bent close to Lance. "None of my business,

Mister, but you better stay clear of this place and Martin Kidd. That's just a friendly warning."

Lance didn't take his eyes off Rose. "Want to tell me why?"

"Just say it's for your own good," Rose said. Then she looked Lance dead in the eye. "What you starin' at?"

Lance stepped back a little, feeling foolish. "Just admirin' your comb. That's quite something."

Rose felt her hair and touched the comb. "That's my protection." She lifted the comb from the mass of red curls and Lance caught a glimpse of the sharp steel blade that held the comb in place.

At that moment the barkeep called to Rose who turned to leave. Then she glanced back at Lance. "Remember what I said about this place and Captain Kidd. You've been warned fairly."

Lance didn't linger in the Cutlass Room. He walked out of the bat-winged doors. He was alert when he did this, not so much from Rose's warning, but because of his encounter with Hap Briley. He doubted the lowlife would be hanging around the lobby of the hotel and further doubted that he would try anything here.

From what Lance had been able to glean from the townsfolk, Briley was in the pocket of the Captain. Lance figured Briley for the type who would bushwack you when you least expected it.

He was glad when he stepped out of the hotel into the brisk, fresh desert air. Lance took a moment to look upward at the spread of blue sky with a now-and-again white cloud. He assured himself once more how much he liked this part of the country and Jubilee in particular.

"So you finally found your way to The Pirate's Den," came a low voice from behind him. Lance craned his neck to see Marshal Crawley standing there.

"Had some business in here, Marshal," Lance said. "Took the time to see for myself just what all the jawin' was about this place."

Crawley rolled a cigarette and touched a match to the tip. "So what do you think of it?"

"It's right impressive. Only, just not my style. Wouldn't want to spend any time in there."

Crawley didn't show any reaction one way or the other. Lance got the impression he was just making talk.

"Probably a wise choice."

"You know something I don't?"

Crawley shrugged. "Just passing on some advice. I'd stick to the bowling alley and the Red Gulley if I was you. This place is too rich for your blood."

"Or maybe I just got better taste. Mornin' Marshal," Lance said and headed back toward the store. Crawley ground the cigarette out angrily with the heel of his boot.

"Wise, little smart-ass," Crawley said in disgust. He was angry because Lance could get the better of him in an argument. He sensed that. And he sensed that Lance could outdraw him six ways to Sunday. He would wait until the wise-acre went afoul of the law, which everyone did sooner or later. Then he would deem it a real privilege to slap him in the hoosegow.

That made Crawley feel better and he strode down the boardwalk toward his office. He even sang a few words from one of the popular ditties of the day. He felt better.

" 'There's a time a comin'

Just wait another day.

There's a time a comin'

When things'll go my way.' "

Crawley slapped the side of his legs and laughed outright. If someone had seen him they would have thought that was out of character for the marshal. Crawley never laughed and he rarely, if ever, sang. Really out of character for him.

It was a long but busy week for Lance Jordan. Even though he worked hard for Mr. Denker, he still found time to think about why he had come to Jubilee and for what purpose. He was still looking for Uncle Ephraim. The encouraging bit of news he had gotten from the miner days ago had sparked a renewed interest in his quest.

Lance felt certain Uncle Ephraim was still somewhere in these parts. He felt this was about as far as his uncle had gone. Lance wondered just how much of the townsfolk's money Ephraim had left or if he had squandered it all.

Lance kept his ears open for any words that might come his way about Uncle Ephraim. It would be several weeks before the miner came back for supplies, so he had to bide his time. He had been able thus far to keep his mission a secret, mainly because he felt it was nobody's business and secondly he wasn't all that proud of what his uncle had done. Thankfully this sort of thing didn't run in the Jordan family.

On Thursday a letter came from Susan. Lance waited until he had finished his day's work and he was in his room when he read it. Susan wrote of how much she missed him and how soon he would be coming for her. She trusted his judgement that Jubilee was all that he wrote it was. What of his uncle? Had he gotten any closer to finding the man? And she closed with vowing once again her unending love for him.

Lance tucked the letter into the pillowcase beneath his head so that he could sleep on it during the night. He missed Susan and even more since he had gotten the letter. There were women at The Pirate's Den and some he had met along the way of his search, but he hadn't messed with any of them. None of them could come close to his Susan.

Lance's sleep that night was chock full of dreams. Dreams of Susan and himself in all kinds of situations. He awoke the next morning with renewed vigor to find his uncle, get the money, and go back to San Anselmo for Susan. He didn't think he could wait much longer.

"Inventory's comin' up, Son," Harley said when Lance came into the store that morning.

"Great. Just tell me what to do."

Harley took a deep swallow of the coffee he was

drinking. "Don't know whether I've told you before, but I'm right pleased with the way you picked up on everything around here."

Lance knew that Harley wasn't used to paying compliments. He just shook his head to thank the older man and got to work stocking the shelves.

"Funny thing," Harley said. "I ain't seen Benny around here lately. You don't suppose that bully Hap Briley scared him off?"

Lance didn't know. "Ought to go check on him one of these days over at the ranch," Harley went on. "But I reckon Ben Taggart would let us know if something was wrong. He keeps a hawk's eye on the boy."

"Maybe I'll ride out after work to see how Benny's doing," Lance said.

"Glad you said that," Harley said in a relieved tone of voice. "Was aimin' to ask you to do that."

Lance chuckled. "Been working here so long I can almost read your mind."

"Just bein' neighborly," Harley replied half seriously. "Besides you need to get out of town for a while anyway."

"What's this about Lance leaving town?" Tom Abbott said, who had come into the store while Harley and Lance had been talking.

"Mornin' Tom," Lance said. "I was just telling Mr. Denker I'm going to ride over to Ben Taggart's spread and see how Benny is getting along. He hasn't been around for his horehound lately."

Tom put one booted foot on the bottom rung of the

ladder Lance was standing on. "Heard about what happened between you and Hap Briley. I'd be watching my back if I was you, Lance. That Briley doesn't care how he brings a man down, just as long as he does."

Again Lance restrained himself from telling Tom about Hap Briley's ambush a few nights ago. That was because Harley was there and Lance didn't think it would do the old man any good to hear about that.

"I'll be careful," Lance said. "What can we do for you, Tom?"

"Not for me, but you. Harriett wants you to come for supper Saturday night. Told me to make an invite when I came to town."

The thought of having a home-cooked meal was mighty appealing to Lance. "I'll be there. You just tell me what time and how to get to your place."

"Come on down from up there, Son," Harley said. "You can't carry on a decent conversation when you got your head in the clouds."

Lance climbed down and Tom Abbott gave him directions to his ranch.

"Should I bring anything? Beans, something like that?" Lance asked. Back in San Anselmo it was understood when you accepted an invite, you brought something along with you.

"Just you and your appetite," Tom said. "Harriett's doing something special with a chicken."

Tom had a list of provisions and Lance filled the order. He told Tom about going into The Pirate's Den. "Quite a fancy place."

"Wouldn't be caught dead in there myself," Tom answered. A wry smile cut the edge of his mouth. "Only, I hear a lot of men have been found in that situation over there."

Harley limped over to the counter. "Keeps Saw Hogan busy writing up those phony death certificates."

Lance was all ears. "Phony?"

Harley made a guttural sound. "Sure as shootin'. Everybody in town knows Saw and the Captain are in cahoots. Someone passes away under unusual circumstances over there and Saw makes everything nice and legal."

"Is that the truth?" Lance was very interested. He was learning more about the nefarious goings on in the infamous Pirate's Den.

"Cal Gordon tells me it is. Cal has two of his young 'uns in one of Harriett's classes. He's the clerk at the Den."

Lance remembered seeing the clerk over there. He had been friendly enough to show him where the Cutlass Room was and that Lance could find Martin Kidd there.

"Anytime you need anything from Cal, just tell him I said it was all right," Tom said, confidently. "Cal's really too honest to be working in a place like that, but he has to make a living and Kidd pays good wages."

All three men heard the commotion at the same time. It came from outside the store. There was yelling and some folks came stomping past on the boardwalk outside. Lance and Tom ran to the front door with Harley hobbling behind them.

Lance stopped Orie Tybolt who was passing by the front of the store. "What's going on, Orie? What's all the ruckus?"

Orie pointed down the street. "Somethin's happened to little Benny. Look down yonder!"

Lance looked in the direction Orie had pointed. He saw a mule lumbering up the street with a lumpy sack tied across its back. Only the sack wasn't that at all. On closer scrutiny Lance saw the head of Benny slowly, lifelessly bounce up and down to the slow cadence of the mule's gait.

"Come on," Lance said, and Tom was at his side as they ran from the store into the street and down to where the mule was. Tom grabbed the animal by the head and steadied it as Lance worked on the ropes that bound the lifeless body to the back of the animal.

Slowly and carefully Lance lowered Benny's body to the street. Orie and his wife had by that time joined the two men.

"He's been shot," Lance said as he held up one of his blood-stained hands. "In the back too."

Orie's wife sobbed as she lifted Benny's head and cradled it in her lap. "He was just a child," she said, as she brushed the street dust out of his hair and off his face.

"What a rotten thing to do," Orie said. "We'd better tell Ben Taggart about this."

Some townspeople had gathered around now. Lance

spoke to the closest one. "Get Saw Hogan or the doctor."

"I'll run for Marshal Crawley," another man said, before he bolted away.

Harley had hobbled up to them by now and he put a hand on Lance's wide shoulders to steady himself as he crouched down.

"Benny never bothered nobody. Who ever done this ought to be strung up. That's the God-certain truth."

"Who would do somethin' like this?" a woman asked. "What's this town coming to?"

"We ought to ride out to Ben Taggart's place, Lance. He ought to be told about this. He cared for Benny like he was one of his own."

Tom said he would wait for the marshal and Lance and Harley moved away from the crowd toward the hitch rail where their horses were tethered. Lance leaped onto his horse and waited while Harley mounted his with some difficulty. As they headed down Main Street, they passed Marshal Crawley who was walking toward the crowd that had gathered around Benny's dead body.

"Anybody see anything?" Crawley asked them. "Anybody got any idea who done this?"

"Maybe," Lance said and he spurred his bay gelding on with Harley keeping up on his sorrel.

Nothing was said between the two men until they reached the outskirts of town.

"What'd you mean back there?"

"About what?"

"About an idea on who shot Benny."

"I got one."

Harley spat some tobacco juice. "I know that. What I want to know is who. Only I kinda got a guess as to who you mean. There was only one man mean enough to pick on little Benny."

Lance shifted in his saddle. "That's right. Hap Briley."

"One thing we got to do is prove it. Won't be easy."

"I know. Only I don't give up easy."

The Taggart ranch was about a half hour's ride from Jubilee. By the time they got there Lance had told Harley about the pot-shot Briley had taken at him while the owner of the store had been in Tucson. Lance felt that the killing of Benny was Briley's way of getting even with Lance for the humiliation he had heaped upon him the day he picked on the slow-witted, young hired hand.

Ben Taggart, a great bear of a man with a bushy beard and a booming voice, met them as they rode up to the ranch. When Harley told him what had happened, Taggart swore and his face got livid.

"Who the hell would do that to a harmless drover like Benny? He never done anyone a minute's hurt his whole life. Wait till I saddle up. I'm riding back with you."

As Taggart walked away, Lance thought he saw the man run his shirt sleeve across his cheeks. It was the only grieving Ben Taggart would allow himself for the lost hired hand.

Heading back to Jubilee, Taggart asked, "Who done it? The marshal got him jailed?"

"Don't know yet who shot Benny," Lance said. "He just came into town strapped to the back of a mule."

Taggart kept his eyes straight ahead. He never once looked at either Lance or Harley. "Sent Benny out on that mule this morning. He was always falling off any of my mustangs and hurting himself. Thought the mule would be more to his liking."

Harley leaned to the side to get a better look at Taggart. "Benny got any kinfolks around these parts?"

Taggart shook his bushy head. "None he spoke of. Far as I know, he was a foundling." Taggart said this in as gentle a tone of voice as he could. Then he said, "If I get my hands on whoever done this, he'll be cougar bait when I get through with him."

"Let the marshal handle it, Ben," Harley said.

"Marshal! He don't care about nothin' except polishin' that tin badge of his. I wouldn't rely on him to churn butter."

Lance felt that it was better if he said nothing about Hap Briley to Ben Taggart, considering the mood the man was in. If it wasn't Hap Briley who killed Benny Taggart, he would be just as guilty of murder if he shot the lowlifer instead of the real killer.

The three rode the rest of the way to Jubilee in silence. But each man was doing some heavy thinking.

When they got to town, the crowd had dispersed.

Tom Abbott was standing in front of the store. Ben Taggart didn't dismount. "Where's Benny?" he growled in an angry voice.

"Saw Hogan's got him over at his place," Tom said. "I'm sorry about Benny, Taggart."

Ben nodded without saying anything. He reined his horse and headed over to Hogan's funeral parlor. After he had gone, Harley said, "He's takin' it bad. No tellin' what he's aimin' on doing."

Harley got off his horse and Lance slowly eased himself out of the saddle. "If you don't need me for a spell, I think I'll go see the marshal," Lance said.

"Things is quiet. If I need you, I know how to reach you."

"I'd better get back to the ranch," Tom said. "Harriett'll need to know about this when she gets home from school." Tom got onto his pinto. "As far as Saturday night goes, Lance, that's still on. We gotta continue, you know."

"Sure," Lance said. "I'll be there."

Tom rode off and Lance waited until Harley had gone into the store before he headed toward Marshal Crawley's office. Lance's anger at what had happened to Benny had slowly subsided, now he was thinking with clear, calm reason. He saw The Pirate's Den ahead and wondered if Hap Briley was hiding out in there.

Lance walked into the marshal's office and saw Crawley sitting at his desk with his booted feet planted on the desk top. Seeing Jordan, a frown started between his thick eyebrows and rose to his forehead which had grown longer with the thining of his hair.

"Jordan! What brings you here?"

"Want to talk to you, Marshal. Want to ask a few questions."

Crawley didn't move from his chair. He waved an arm to Lance motioning toward an office chair. "Take a seat. Might as well be comfortable."

"I'll stand. What you aimin' on doing about Benny's murder? You going after who shot him?"

"I'm working on it," Crawley said as he stretched his arms and put his hands behind his head.

"Is this the way they work on murders up in Wyoming?" Lance couldn't keep the sarcasm out of his voice.

It didn't seem to make a dent in Crawley's self-assured attitude. He just smiled at Lance. "You know you really ought to just mind your own business and take care of the store. You're no more'n a stranger here in Jubilee."

"I would mind my business, but it looks to me like the law around here won't let me," Lance shot back. The barb found its mark. Marshal Crawley yanked his legs from off the desk after he had lowered his arms.

"Something about you, Jordan, gets to me," he said. "You came into town just lookin' for trouble."

Lance held his ground. He just stared at the marshal and didn't once blink or flinch. This infuriated Crawley even more. He couldn't figure Jordan out and he didn't know how to handle him.

"I'll find Benny's killer," Crawley said. "You just stay out of my way while I'm doing it."

Lance calmly said, "Just what I wanted to hear, Marshal. Benny was well-liked around here. I take his killing really personal."

"You get in my way and I'll slam you behind bars," Crawley said.

"Then I'll remember to stay out of your way. Afternoon, Marshal."

Lance walked out of the office and Marshal Crawley slammed the door shut behind him. Lance had no respect for Crawley. He was like the town bully who backed down when called and his cowardly streak didn't hide itself. Lance knew Crawley wouldn't do anything about Benny's killing. He would strut around town and make a good showing. In time he would hope the whole thing would be forgotten. Only Lance didn't aim on letting Benny's death be forgotten. He felt that Crawley knew that too, that's why he had gotten so riled back there.

Crawley watched Lance walk away from behind the plate glass window. He beat his fist against the door in anger and frustration. Why did he let that scum of a man get to him like this? He looked at his fist that was raw and bleeding then went away to wash the blood off his knuckles.

Saturday was a busy day for Lance at the store. By late afternoon, business slackened and Harley closed up a little early.

"So, you can get yourself lookin' respectable to go to supper."

Lance filled the tub with scalding water that nearly took the hide off his body. He put on a clean chambray shirt and his best plaid vest and pulled on his fifty-dollar boots. All this he did as etiquette, not for Tom Abbott who couldn't have cared how Lance looked, but for Harriett.

Before riding out of town, Lance rode over to Saw Hogan's to make sure Benny had a good pine box to be buried in.

"Don't you worry any," Hogan said. "Ben Taggart is taking care of all the arrangements. He's going to pay for a fine coffin for Benny. He chose it himself, just this afternoon. Want a peek at him? If I say so myself I've done a first-rate job on him. Now and then a man's got to brag on himself."

Lance would rather had not seen Benny, but out of respect he went and viewed the remains. He didn't tarry long in the slumber room but got on his gelding and headed for the Abbott place.

In all the excitement of the past few days he had almost forgotten about Uncle Ephraim. Riding through the gathering dusk he had time to once again remind himself of his mission.

It was getting on toward sundown and the clouds in the west were a brilliant orange and a pale shade of purple. There was a slight breeze and it felt good after the heat of the day.

Lance was passing through a stand of trees when

the first shot rang out. The bullet whined past his head and nicked the brim of his Stetson.

With lightning reaction Lance bent over double so he wouldn't be a target and his hand spun his Colt .45 from its holster and he waited until he saw the flash from the barrel of the bushwhacker's gun. Lance's six-shooter roared as he emptied the chamber of the gun.

Chapter Five

Lance spurred his gelding, who responded by galloping furiously along the well-beaten trail through the trees. By now it had gotten well-bottom dark and Lance let his horse have his head. Even if he couldn't see that well in the darkness, his horse seemed to not hesitate in dashing along the pathway until they were out of the woods.

This time, Lance wasn't sure who the shooter might have been. Hap Briley was the logical first choice since he had tried before. But, would he have tried so soon after taking Benny's life? Even though Lance had no proof the killer of Benny was Hap Briley, he couldn't think of anyone else who might have been mean enough to have done it.

For a fleeting moment, he thought about Marshal Crawley. Not for a St. Louis minute did he believe the marshal wasn't capable of a bushwhack. After his encounter with him that day, Lance felt he hadn't exactly made a life-long friend out of the marshal.

With one quick glance back over his shoulder, Lance satisfied himself that he wasn't being pursued. He realized now that he should have been more aware, more on his guard. But he had let thoughts of Uncle Ephraim take his mind off his natural alertness. From now on, he would have to be constantly vigilant, constantly as aware as a coyote on a scent.

When he got to the Abbott's, Tom was in front of the small, well-built little house cutting kindling. Tom took one final swing with his ax, expertly splitting the chunk of firewood in half.

"Right on time, Lance," Tom said. "Thought I heard gunfire out there. You see anything?"

Lance lowered his tall frame from his horse. "Someone took a few shots at me. Just as I was coming through that grove of trees."

Tom moved quickly over to Lance. "You all right? Did you see who did it?"

Lance took off his Stetson. There was a bullet hole in the brim.

"Too dark to see who it was. Have a feeling it might be Hap Briley, maybe somebody else."

"Sounds like the way he'd handle things, that Briley. Probably still got his back up on account of you bestin' him in front of the store."

Harriett came outside and stood in the doorway. "Is

that you, Lance? Why don't the two of you come inside. Supper's just about ready."

"Be right there," Tom said. "I'll wash up out here."

Lance followed Tom over to the pump where he
dredged up some ice-chilled water and splashed it on
his face and hands. Drying his hands and face on a
hunk of torn muslin, he said to Lance, "Let's not say
anything to Harriett about this until after supper."

"I hear you. No need to upset her. Knowing your
wife I would figure she's been working on this supper
for a while."

Together they went inside the warm house. Harriett
had set a nice table. She had used the damask table-
cloth that had been a wedding gift from her mother
and the new, unchipped dishware Tom had bought on
their tenth wedding anniversary.

"Everything looks just great," Lance said. "I see
what I've been missing since I left San Anselmo."

"Please be seated," Harriett said, beaming with pleasure. Tom pulled a chair out for his wife and Lance
sat down opposite her. The food looked and smelled
delicious to Lance who had been subsisting on whatever he could buy at Denker's store and sometimes
purchasing a meal at the Red Gulley.

Tom, as the perfect host with manners drilled into
him after months of coaching by his patient wife,
headed the table. He passed the chicken, the gravy, the
biscuits, the mashed potatoes, and the beans almadine
with such casualness that Lance wasn't aware that he

had once had a bunkhouse reach and manners to go along with it.

Harriett insisted Tom say grace and then Lance bit into a piece of the succulent chicken. Harriett got up from the table for the coffee pot and as she filled her husband's and Lance's cups she said, "Now, what was all that gunfire I heard just before you rode up, Lance? I know you, Tom Abbott, you want to protect me from hearing any distressing news."

Tom just shook his head as he ladled some giblet gravy onto a mound of mashed potatoes. "Lance said someone got off some shots at him when he was coming through that stand of oaks just south of here."

"I see," Harriett said. "Does that have anything to do with your fracas with Mr. Briley, Lance?"

Lance lifted one eyebrow at what Harriett said.

"No, Tom said nothing about it. This is a small, tight community, Lance. Word somehow manages to get around. I commend you on doing what you did to Mr. Briley. He is a bully and an insensitive man. Poor little Benny. What a sad end he came to."

"I believe it was either Hap Briley who fired the gun, or, maybe, some other drover. I don't want to accuse anybody. Not until I have proof."

Tom reached for another biscuit and lathered it with creamy butter. "You said that before, Lance. Who else has it in for you?"

"I'll just keep that to myself, Tom. Maybe I'm not right, maybe I am. Don't want you mixed up in this."

"Why not?" Harriett said. "I hope you can trust us. We are friends, are we not?"

Lance had to concede that. He just didn't want any harm to come to either Harriett or Tom, so he felt it was better if they knew as little as possible about his words with Marshal Crawley.

"You are friends," Lance said. "And I care about that. When I know something more, I'll tell you. Believe me."

"You know best," Tom said. "Let's let Lance do things his way. We just want you to know we're here for you, Lance, whenever you need us."

"Thanks, I 'preciate that."

That settled, they ate the rest of the meal while just getting to know each other. Lance learned that Harriett was from a good, prosperous family in New York. Tom had met her through a mutual acquaintance.

"I'd always had a desire to live and work in the Southwest," Harriett said. "Marrying Tom was like a dream come true."

"So, now it comes out," Tom said and winked at Lance. "You only married me to get a free ride to Arizona."

Harriett was quick to figure out that Tom was just showing off in front of company. "Oh, yes. I'm still trying to find out how I can get back to New York. Everything looks the same out here in the wilds of Arizona."

Tom realized he had been bested and he held up his

hands. "Peace! At all costs. What about you, Lance. How did you end up in Jubilee?"

Lance decided he could trust the Abbotts. Besides, they didn't know Uncle Ephraim or any of the folks in San Anselmo.

"I came here looking for my uncle. I've been tracking him ever since he left New Mexico. Finally met someone the other day who shed some light on Uncle Ephraim. He just might be here in Jubilee."

"You came all this way to find your uncle?" Tom asked. "Something you ain't tellin' us about him, Lance?"

It all came out then. All about the fire that had wiped out a family leaving them with nothing but the clothes on their backs. How he had made a vow that he would find his uncle and bring him and the money back to San Anselmo.

"There ain't never been any thief or criminal that I know of in the Jordan side of the family," Lance said. "What Uncle Ephraim did isn't something you go around braggin' about."

Tom and Harriett listened with great interest. They, like so many others who came in contact with the handsome six-footer, were taken by him. He had an openness and an honesty about him that came through.

"Once you find your uncle," Harriett said. "I suppose you'll be taking him back to New Mexico."

"It's my plan. I just hope he hasn't spent all the money that was collected."

Tom took a sip of coffee. "This miner, the one you

said spoke to you about your uncle, has he been back in town?"

Lance shook his head. "I've been waitin' and watchin' for him. Don't know if he told me all he knows about Uncle Ephraim or not. But I have a hunch that if Uncle Ephraim did come to Jubilee, there's only one place he would hang out."

"The Pirate's Den," Tom said. "Sounds like you're on the right trail, Lance."

"I think so. Tomorrow I'm going to see Cal Gordon over there and ask him a few questions."

Harriett cut a wedge of the peach pie for Lance and handed it to him on a saucer. "Cal's an honest man. If there's anything on your uncle, he'll tell you, Lance. I've taught his children and he's raised them to be honest in all their dealings."

Tom lifted his cup and finished off the coffee. "If you do find your uncle and take him back to New Mexico, what then? You won't be headed back this way?"

Lance slowly nodded. "I've found a place I want to settle down in. San Anselmo's a good place, only I wasn't sure I wanted to stay there. When I rode into Jubilee that first day, I knew it was what I been lookin' for."

Harriett poured more coffee for Tom. "Anyone special back there in San Anselmo?"

Lance couldn't hide how he felt about Susan, no matter how hard he tried. "She's just about the most perfect female I ever met. She's school learned, she can cook, she's as pretty as a sunrise and she can sit a horse as good as any trail boss."

"Sounds to me as if you made up your mind about not stayin' single," Tom said with mock sincerity. "Better give that a lot of thought. Don't want to go high-tailin' it into somethin' before you give it a lot of serious thought."

"Just like you did, I suppose," Harriett was quick to say. "How long did you know me before you proposed? Let's see . . . four days as I count it."

Lance laughed as Tom reached for one more slice of peach pie.

In the dark, the lone man rode toward Jubilee. He clutched the reins of his horse with his right hand. The wound in his left shoulder was bleeding badly and was burning like hot fire even though he had stuffed a kerchief inside his shirt.

His aim had been off tonight, he didn't know what the problem was. Lately he found his eyesight played tricks on him. It worried him. In his line of work, that could be more than just a liability, it could mean a death sentence. He tried not to think about the pain but it throbbed and he knew he had to get to Saw Hogan in a hurry. Saw could be relied upon to do a good job of patching up and not ask any questions.

That Jordan had to be silenced. There was just something about him that spelled real trouble for Jubilee and for his own well-being. The moon came out from behind a cloud bank and the lone rider looked back to see if Jordan had followed. One thing you had to hand to Jordan, he was fast on the draw. Maybe he was a gun tipper and was hiding out in Jubilee. Then the rider winced as a fiery tongue of pain flashed through his arm from the shoulder wound.

Just hang on, he said for comfort. *You'll make it all right. Only the next time it'll be Jordan who has a hole in his body. Not just a nick but a gut wound.*

Under the cover of darkness, he rode into town and right to Saw Hogan's place. Hogan was up and he had an open bottle of raw whiskey that he poured down the lone man's gullet before attacking the wound.

It was late when Lance left the Abbotts. He did so with reluctance. The warm, friendly couple and the cozy, clean house were hard to give up.

"Don't be a stranger," Tom's parting words were. "It's a standing invite."

"We can always make room for you, Lance," Harriett said. "I hope you find your uncle."

Lance urged his horse away from the Abbott's. He made a wide swing around the stand of oaks, even if it was the long way home. Yet, as he rode, he was alert and wary. There was no telling if the bushwhacker was still in there waiting for a chance or not. He breathed easier when he had circled the trees and was on the trail to Jubilee.

There was a full moon tonight and it cast a silvery light on the land. A night wind came moaning from the north and it made a lonesome, chilling sound.

Lance turned up the collar on his jacket and kept glancing from side to side to assure himself he was alone on the trail.

Riding into Jubilee, there were still some coal-oil lamps burning in the homes huddled together on the outskirts of town. He could hear the sound of voices from the Red Gulley and an occasional yell followed by whooping laughter. Otherwise the town was quiet. Nobody was on the street but himself.

Lance guided his gelding into the small corral next to the mercantile store where he gave it a good rub-down after taking off the saddle and blanket.

As he was shutting the gate behind him he heard a voice from out of the darkness. "Have a good time, Son?" It was Harley.

"Shouldn't do that, Harley," Lance said. "Show yourself before you speak to a man."

Harley hobbled out of the shadows. "Why you bein' so testy? Something happen tonight?"

"Someone used me for a little target practice again," Lance said. "Right before I got to the Abbotts."

"You all right?"

"Bad aim. I got off a few rounds. Think I might have winged whoever it was."

"That bein'?"

"Dunno. It was getting pretty dark out there. Don't want to go accusin' someone without any proof."

Harley ground out his cigarette under the heel of his boot. "You're right there. Think I'll head back inside. Gettin' pretty late for this old drover."

Lance walked alongside Harley. Even in such familiar surroundings he was cautious. He might have winged the bushwhacker, but not fatally and he might be waiting to take another try. He put himself between Harley and the protection of the store. If Harley was aware of this he said nothing.

Lance said good night when he got to his room and made sure he didn't cast a shadow on the window while he slipped out of his clothes and between the covers. Strangely, his thoughts were not of the gunman, but of Susan Wells before he drifted off to sleep.

The next day, Lance was restless and uneasy working. Harley noticed this and said, "What's eatin' you, Son?"

"Still thinking about that bushwhacker over there near the Abbotts. I'd like to ride out there and take a look around."

"What you waitin' for?" Harley said. "I'd feel better if I know you didn't have that shootin' on your mind."

As Lance was leaving, he saw Reuben Mundy coming up the boardwalk to the store. Although his clothing was ragged and patched, there was an air of genteel poverty about him. He didn't carry himself like a defeated, broken man. He tipped his hat to Lance as they passed.

Lance saddled up and rode out of town, passing the marshal's office and The Pirate's Den as he moved down Main Street. Crawley wasn't outside, but Lance saw movement behind the plate glass window as though the marshal was watching him but trying to stay hidden.

There was more activity in front of The Pirate's Den with a few patrons tethering their horses at the hitch-rail before swaggering behind the mosaic-glassed doors. Idly, Lance wondered if Hap Briley was inside at one of the tables in the Cutlass Room. He was tempted to go inside and surprise the lowlife dog, but decided there would be time enough later to do that.

Lance spurred his gelding who trotted the short distance out of town. For the rest of the way to the stand of oak trees, Lance just rode along taking in the countryside around him and wondering what he would find when he got to where he had been shot at. He also mulled over in his mind the toss-up between Hap Briley and Marshal Crawley. It was a problem with Lance since he spent a good deal of his time making people like him. It came easy to Lance, but he knew from past experience that he couldn't win over everyone.

When he got to the stand of oaks, he brought his horse to a standstill. The gelding snorted and pawed the ground with one of its front hoofs as though sending a signal that it didn't like the area.

Lance slipped out of the saddle and left his horse behind while he walked into the stand of trees. Already the sun was blazing down from a cloudless blue sky, but here in the shade of the overhanging branches it was cool.

Slowly and cautiously, Lance moved through the

underbrush trying not to disturb anything. Then he saw something sparkling from a ray of sunlight filtering through a break in the overhead trees.

Walking closer, he saw that the flash of light came from a spent cartridge shell. He had found where his assailant had fired upon him. There were scuff marks too, made by boots and the unmistakable prints of a shod horse. Lance crouched down searching until he found what he was looking for—telltale brownish splotches on the ground and what foliage there was. He got to his feet satisfied. He had wounded the man. One bullet had found its mark.

Lance turned and headed back for his horse. This should make his search for the bushwhacker easier. Someone with a recent gunshot wound shouldn't be all that hard to find back in Jubilee.

It was around noon when Lance rode back into town. By this time of day the streets were more active with horsemen and wagons and buggies. Townsfolk walked the boardwalks or stayed in the shade cast by the overhanging roofs.

Nearing The Pirate's Den, Lance urged his horse to the hitchrail. He dismounted and went inside. Looking around, he saw people milling about. A few patrons were seated in high-backed, upholstered chairs reading newspapers or magazines.

Cal Gordon was alone at the counter and he recognized Lance and nodded. Lance walked over to the counter. "Remember me? I was talking to Tom and

Harriett Abbott last night. Your name came up and they said you might be able to help me."

At the mention of the Abbotts, Cal nodded eagerly. "Anything I can do, I'll be more than willing."

"I'm looking for a man who might be registered here. His name is Ephraim Jordan. Sound familiar?"

Cal opened the register before him and ran a finger down the pages as he turned them. "How long ago do you think he checked in?"

"A week. Maybe two."

"No Ephraim Jordan here. Look for yourself."

Lance scanned the open pages of the register. He didn't see Uncle Ephraim's name there, but he saw a name that he had heard before. Zeke McDeke. It was so unusual that he couldn't miss it. Nobody had a name like that. He thanked Cal and then headed for the Cutlass Room.

At this time of the day, as before, there were few patrons at the bar so it was easy for Lance to spot Saw Hogan who was leaning his ample girth against the bar while he lifted a glass to his lips.

Lance waited until Hogan put down an empty glass before he strolled over.

"Buy you a drink, Mr. Hogan?"

Saw squinted at Lance and then a smile spread across his florid face as recognition set in. "I would deem that a quintessential honor and a rare privilege, Mr. Jordan."

"I take it that means yes," Lance motioned for a refill.

Saw accepted the newly acquired drink and took an experimental sip before cradling it in his hands.

They talked for a few minutes about the weather, the nation's political bent, and then Lance casually said, "Imagine you get a lot of drop-in cases, Mr. Hogan. Snake bites, accidents, gunshot wounds."

Before answering, this required a hefty swallow by Hogan of his drink. "Every day it's something. Why just last night I treated a man for a gunshot wound. Shoulder shot, just missed the bone but there was a lot of bleeding."

Lance was very interested.

"Sounds serious. Wonder who that could have been?"

Hogan finished his drink and Lance made a motion to the barkeep for another refill. Hogan raised it in a toast to Lance and said, " ' . . . the physician after long putting off gives the silent and terrible look for an answer . . .'. " He took a long pull on the drink. Then he smacked his lips and looked at Hogan. "Where were we?"

Lance was anxious to learn who the man was Hogan had treated last night, but he didn't want to appear too eager. "Something about one of your patients. Someone with a gunshot wound."

A light came into Hogan's eyes and he was about to speak when they were interrupted by Martin Kidd.

"Need to talk to you, Hogan. . . . right now!"

Chapter Six

"You will excuse us, Jordan," the Captain said as he put a tight grip on Hogan's arm and led him away.

Lance watched the two as they left the Cutlass Room. Saw Hogan had miraculously become sober and he was listening closely to what the owner of The Pirate's Den had to say to him.

When they had gone, Lance looked around hoping to see Hap Briley, but he was nowhere to be seen. He paid the barkeep and walked out of the room.

Outside he got on his gelding and rode the short distance to the store. There were a few customers inside and Lance got to work lifting the heavy sacks of grain and boxes of supplies for Harley.

As they worked, Harley asked, "Did you find anything out? Any trace of who took a shot at you?"

"Found a few cartridges and some blood stains."

Harley chuckled. "So you winged the buzzard. Good shootin', Lance."

That was about all that Lance could or wanted to share with the owner of the mercantile store. He harbored a protective feeling toward the older man. No use burdening him with his problems. Harley was good enough to take him on as a hired hand without knowing a flying hawk thing about him.

Around 3:00 Orie Tybolt came in to announce that there would be a funeral tomorrow for Benny.

"After all these years we don't even know his last name," the soft-spoken rancher said. "Seems a shame that he'll only have that one name on his tombstone."

"I'll bring some flowers from my garden," a plain woman in a bonnet said, as she dabbed at a tear on her cheek. "There have to be flowers."

"You going?" Harley asked when the store was less crowded.

"Planning to. You want to come along?"

"I liked little Benny. I want to go."

That was all that was said about the funeral. The rest of the day, Lance kept a quick eye on the street outside the store. The drovers who were getting fired up at The Pirate's Den had drifted noisily from the hotel to the Red Gulley which was closer to the store.

Every once in a while a wild, ear-splitting yelp went up, sometimes followed by a blast from someone's sixshooter.

"Doesn't Marshal Crawley ever do anything about that?" Lance asked Harley.

James Rhodes

Harley was mopping up and he just shook his head. "Crawley's probably hidin' out like a treed cougar. He's all talk. Known that for sometime now."

"Why doesn't somebody do something about him?" Lance grunted, as he moved a keg of briny pickles.

"We hired him, voted him into office. Now looks like we're stuck with the man."

Lance stayed close to the store the rest of the day just in case those liquored-up cowhands decided to ride into the place, just for kicks.

Lance didn't sleep well that night. It might have been because of the noise of the cowpokes who didn't leave town until well after midnight. Or it may have been that something was troubling him. Something he had seen that day that clung to the back of his mind like ticks to a bear.

He had a few cups of hot, scalding coffee, Harley's specialty that Lance was certain was made from lye and coal dust, the next morning. This brought him around and left him wide awake. Even though he was working hard that morning and helping Harley in whatever needed to be done, that nagging feeling of yesterday still hung over him like a thundercloud.

They broke for dinner at noon and Harley closed up the store and took Lance to Hoonahan's for something to eat. "It's on me. Been meaning to spring for a meal ever since you got into town."

Hoonahan's was just on the next block. It was not fancy, almost ugly would be a better description, but the food was good and wholesome.

Harley introduced Lance to Monte Hoonahan, the rotund, friendly owner with muttonchop whiskers. Hoonahan gave Lance a powerful handshake and said, "Special of the day coming up."

"What's the special of the day?" Lance asked.

"Same as it is every day, steak and taters," Hoonahan said in a booming voice. Then he leaned over the table and said in a lower voice, "Only thing we ever serve." He gave Lance a wink and went off to fix their order.

"Quite a drover," Lance said and he smiled for the first time in a while.

"Hoonahan's as honest as they come. Says what's on his mind. And you get your money's worth."

Lance looked around at the noonday crowd. Not the kind of people you would see at either The Pirate's Den or Red Gulley. These were local townsfolk. Hard working, honest citizens who knew each other and felt this was their place just as the wild drovers and the hard-living gunslingers felt at ease in The Den and Red Gulley's.

Hoonahan brought their food on huge spitting platters. A steak the size of a side of buffalo and half the potato crop of country Cork looked up at Lance. Once more Harley was right.

"Closing up after the noon meal," Hoonahan said. "Me and the missus are going to the funeral."

"We're already closed," Harley said. "All of those people coming too?"

Hoonahan looked around. "As soon as they finish

eatin'. Going to be quite a gathering out there on Piute Street."

Lance cut into his steak and lifted the cut portion to his mouth. It was cooked just the way he liked it.

"Haven't had a steak this good since I left San Anselmo," Lance said, spearing some fried potatoes sprinkled with onions.

"New Mexico, huh," Hoonahan said. "Fine part of the country that San Anselmo is."

"Been there?" Lance asked.

"Quite a few times. Feller was in here a while back from over there. Funny thing meeting two people from the same small town in such a short space of time."

Lance quit eating. He looked closely at Monte Hoonahan and asked, "Did this feller have a name? Might know him from back home."

Hoonahan leaned on the back of an empty chair while he thought for a moment. Then he pushed his lower lip forward with his tongue before he said, "Can't recollect he did. Older man, kept eyeing his horse and saddle bag through the window all the time he was in here. Do remember he left a mighty generous tip."

It had to be Uncle Ephraim, Lance thought. It was just too much of a coincidence that someone else fitting his description would be passing through Jubilee.

Hoonahan left their table to attend to the other customers. Harley looked at Lance and said, "You hardly been touchin' that steak. What's the matter?"

Lance shook off the thoughts of Uncle Ephraim and

bent over the steak cutting a thick, juicy slice. He lifted it to his mouth and chewed on it, enjoying the succulent flavor. Then he said, "Nothin's the matter. Just being polite to Hoonahan."

They ate their dinner and then Hoonahan refilled their cups with coffee.

"What time did Tybolt say the burial was?" Harley asked as he finished his coffee.

"Noon. Should be getting over there right now," Lance answered, shoving his chair back and rising to his feet.

"Be right there," Harley said, slowly standing up. "Want to pay Hoonahan for the meal."

"Meet you outside."

"Shouldn't be but a minute."

"I'll be waiting."

Stepping outside, Lance met Tom and Harriett who had come to town in their buggy. "Want a ride over to the cemetery, Lance?" Tom offered.

"I'm waitin' for Harley. He's inside paying for the food."

"We've got room for two more," Harriett said. "Why don't the both of you join us. It's better than you walking over to the cemetery."

"Thanks, Harriett, I think Harley would like that. Here he comes now."

Lance told the older man what had been offered. He said, "Much obliged," and heaved himself into the buggy as Lance lifted himself in beside him.

They rode out of town, past The Pirate's Den and

Lance saw Martin Kidd standing in the doorway of the hotel watching the buggy as it passed by. He wondered to himself what part the Captain had in the killing of defenseless Benny.

"That's a waste of human flesh," Harley put into words what each of them were secretly thinking. "Worst thing in the world when that hotel got built in Jubilee."

"It brought in a lot of people," Tom said.

"Wrong kind," was Harley's assessment.

Lance kept quiet. He had his own thinking to do. He had to find out about the man Saw Hogan doctored last night for gunshot wounds. If Kidd hadn't come by when he did, Lance was certain Hogan would have spit out the man's name.

As they got to the cemetery they were joined by the townsfolk. Lance saw that Benny must have been well thought of among these people. He later learned that most of them never knew the slow-witted boy. He had become something to them, something that drew them all together as a community to show their solidarity against the forces that would do this sort of thing to someone as helpless and defenseless as Benny.

When they got to the cemetery the crowd had grown to a considerable size. A lot of the menfolk were standing there more to please their wives than to make any kind of statement.

Tom helped Harriett out of the buggy and Lance

and Harley walked beside them and stood respectfully at a distance from the burial site.

Ben Taggart and his men were gathered around the open plot of land. There was a chilly northern wind blowing and the sky was overcast with heavy, bloated clouds. It was a somber scene and those gathered drew together for comfort and protection against the wind.

While the congregational preacher was reading from the bible, Lance glanced around at the faces of the people. He was surprised to see one face at the rear of the crowd who didn't belong there.

At the same time Harley saw the man.

He whispered to Lance, "What's that lowlife Kidd doin' here? He never cared for Benny. Didn't even know him as far as I recollect."

Before Lance could answer, the pastor asked them to join in the singing of a hymn. Lance's lilting tenor was drowned out by Harley's loud, off-key baritone. It was so bad that several of the nearest mourners moved several paces away.

After the singing there was a brief eulogy by the pastor and the service ended.

As the people moved away, Ben Taggart spotted Martin Kidd standing in the same place on the out-skirts of the crowd. Boldly, he walked over to the Captain.

"You ain't wanted here, Mr. Kidd. For all I know you might have had a hand in Benny's killing. It would be just like you to do something like that."

Martin Kidd didn't appear to be in the least bit intimidated by Ben Taggart even though the rancher out-weighed him by fifty pounds.

"I won't hold this against you, Taggart," the Captain said evenly. "Knowing that you are just not yourself today."

Ben Taggart's face flamed with rage and pent-up anger. His hands tightened into great, hard fists and it looked to Lance as though the big man was about to tangle with the Captain.

At that moment Marshal Crawley stepped forward. Lance hadn't seen him at the burial so he must have just gotten there. Crawley stood between the two of them. Only his badge kept Taggart from doing what he had intended.

"Ben," Crawley said, "this is a burial. Don't forget where you are. All this can wait until another time."

Taggart was looking at the star pinned on Crawley's shirt. He never cared much for the marshal but he did respect the law and that was the only thing that stayed his hand.

"There'll be other times, Kidd," Taggart said ve-hemently. "I won't forget what happened to Benny. Somebody is gonna pay for that."

With one final glance at the Captain, Taggart turned and walked away to where his family was gathered, waiting for him. He didn't turn back, but hustled everyone into his wagon and snapped the reins head-ing the team of horses out of town.

Crawley turned to Martin Kidd and said, "Real sorry about that, Mr. Kidd. Ben Taggart had a powerful likin' toward Benny. You've got to overlook what he said."

Martin Kidd just smiled and said, "No need to apologize for Taggart, Marshal. He meant what he said. Wouldn't be a bit surprised if he tried to gun me down first chance he gets."

Marshal Crawley didn't like that kind of talk. He also didn't like the crowd that was being attracted. He didn't want to make any disturbance. He liked things to stay peaceful and calm, no matter what the cost.

Martin Kidd turned toward the crowd made up mostly of men and said, "Only way I know to help you people get over this terrible tragedy is to open the bar for you. Come on over to The Den, drinks are on the house. For the memory of poor, little Benny."

It was an offer that none of the men, or at least those whose wives didn't prevent, could refuse. A murmur of approval went up from the crowd who, led by Captain Martin Kidd, left the cemetery to drown their grief and sorrow and do some spirited mourning.

Lance wanted to go; not to drink, but to find out something for himself. "I'm going with them, Harley. I got my reasons."

"Take as long as you like. All my trade is headed in that direction anyway."

Lance walked alone, following the throng down Piute Street. He was remembering, remembering a story Uncle Ephraim had been fond of telling. All about a man named Zeke McDeke and how he had single-handedly dug the Grand Canyon, colored the Painted

Desert and probably was responsible for just about anything that Paul Bunyon had overlooked. It was an amusing story and Uncle Ephraim always used that name whenever he heard about some great feat someone in San Anselmo had accomplished. He called it a "McDeker."

He had not seen Uncle Ephraim's name on the register at the hotel. But he had seen Zeke McDeke. Only Uncle Ephraim would use that name as a disguise. The odds of a real Zeke McDeke staying at the Pirate's Den in the town of Jubilee were about a million pesos to one.

Lance felt that he had finally found his uncle. Now that his search was reaching a conclusion, he was in no hurry to find the man and bring him back to San Anselmo for justice to be served. First, he would find Uncle Ephraim, confront him about the stolen money, get the money, if there was anything left, and put it in a safe place. Then he would think about bringing him back to New Mexico.

The talk ahead of him was about what a right-acting man Martin Kidd was.

"Guess I was mistaken about him," a man said.

"Same goes for me. Better not believe everything you hear about a killer."

Strange how you can win folks over, Lance thought. *Even with just the offer of a few drink of rotgut.*

Lance stayed at a distance from the rest of the men, waiting his chance to go up the stairs at the hotel. He remembered the room number he had seen in the register that had been assigned to Zeke McDeke. A silly name, Lance thought. Uncle Ephraim should have known better.

When the crowd got to the hotel, Captain Kidd stood at the batwing doors leading to the Cutlass Room and personally shook the hand of each man who passed by.

Being so occupied, he didn't see Lance slip away from the crowd and walk boldly up the staircase to the second floor where the rooms for the tenants were.

Down the carpeted hallway Lance could see the room numbers and Uncle Ephraim would be in the third room on the right. Lance heard some voices from below and saw two men coming up the stairs. He looked around and spotted a closet door that was standing open. Lance moved quickly to the closet and squeezed inside. He reached out and brought the door towards him, leaving it open a crack so that he could see what was going on.

The two men lingered at the top of the stairs finishing their cigars. They were talking cattle and freight yards. Lance only half listened to their palaver. He was thinking about Uncle Ephraim and why, if he was at the hotel, he hadn't run into him even the short time he had been in Jubilee.

The men finally finished their cigars and one went down the hallway to a room while the other came near the closet and then opened the door opposite and went inside. Lance waited a few more minutes to make sure the two didn't come out of their rooms again. When he was satisfied, he cautiously opened the closet door and slipped out into the hallway.

Now he headed in the direction of Uncle Ephraim's room. As he passed the stairs he could hear the muffled sound of men's voices coming from below. There was no laughter amid the din because, after all, this was the day they had buried little, inoffensive Benny.

Lance came to the room Uncle Ephraim had been assigned. He stood there for a few moments thinking. He had come to the end of his search. On the other side of that door would be the man he had been looking for all those weeks. He raised his hand to knock on the door but stopped in midair. From within he heard the sound of voices. Someone was with Uncle Ephraim. He had found someone along the way from San Anselmo to confide in.

It was now or never for Lance. He brought his fist down hard against the door and pounded about five times.

"Who's there?" a muffled man's voice said from inside. It must be Uncle Ephraim. Only it didn't sound like him. Nobody came to the door.

Lance banged on the door again not answering the question that had been asked.

"Hold your pants on," came another voice. It was a woman's voice. Unmistakably a woman's voice and there was anger in the tone.

Lance stepped back and waited. The door was flung open and the woman who he had seen the first time he had come to the hotel stood there. The flash from the gemstones in the comb sticking up from her hair matched the anger in her eyes.

"You should know better than to interrupt a lady while she's working."

"Sorry, ma'am," Lance said feeling awkward and tongue-tied. "I was lookin' for someone. Guess maybe I got the wrong room."

"I'd say you did," came a man's voice from within. Lance saw a man standing in the middle of the room wearing a Stetson and longjohns. "Go find your own room."

Lance backed even farther away. By this time Rose had regained some of her good humor and dignity back. "What's this drover's name you're lookin' for, Hon?"

Lance didn't think that would help matters any so he said, "Just someone I know. I can see he isn't here. I'll check with the desk check again."

"Good idea."

"Sorry again."

"Just a mix-up. Could happen to anybody."

Lance moved even farther away from the door. The drover in the longjohns walked over to Rose and took her by the arm. With his other hand he slammed the door shut.

Lance shook his head and looked down the hallway. Several folks had their heads poked out of their open doors and were eyeing him suspiciously. Lance just smiled and nodded and they all withdrew without saying a word and shut the doors behind them.

As quickly as he could, Lance quick-stepped down the hallway and was relieved when he came to the head of the stairs. Going down them as rapidly as he could, he immediately wondered what had happened to Uncle Ephraim. He hadn't been wrong. That was the room number he had seen written after Uncle Ephraim's name in the register.

At the foot of the stairs Lance stopped. To his right was the Cutlass Room, and this close, the voices from the men inside became clearer. There still wasn't much laughter, but they weren't exactly in deep mourning either.

Shaking his head Lance walked over to the desk where Cal was sorting some letters.

"Quite a celebration going on in there," Lance said.

Cal just shook his head. "Benny deserves better."

Lance got right to the point. He told Cal about knowing this McDeke person but he wasn't in the room assigned to him.

"McDeke?" Cal's eyebrows rose. "He's not in that room anymore. Got a man from Chicago checked in."

"Where did McDeke move to?"

Cal stopped sorting the letters and looked directly at Lance before he said, "Boot Hill. Died a while back, in his sleep."

Chapter Seven

"Died? Are you sure?" Lance was stunned by the news. He couldn't believe Uncle Ephraim was dead. "Maybe you got him mixed up with someone else."

Cal opened the register and ran an expert finger down the list of names. "Nope. Mr. McDeke was in that room. Now it says a Mr. Shaver from Chicago checked in to that room yesterday."

Lance was too confused and disappointed to say anything. He just stood there looking at the open pages of the register.

"Was this McDeke a good friend of yours, Mr. Jordan?" Cal asked in a sympathetic voice.

Lance nodded. "I've known him all my life. I just can't believe he went this way and so quickly."

"You ought to look up Saw Hogan. If I remember he signed the death certificate, and made all the funeral arrangements. He handles all the sudden passings here at The Den."

Lance's interest was piqued.

"Lot of passings here?"

"More'n you would expect."

"Don't that seem kind of peculiar to you?"

Cal closed the book. "Never worked in a hotel before. Can't really say how many people die in hotel rooms. You gotta remember, Mr. Jordan, lots of people pass by this desk in a year's time."

He was probably right, Lance thought. Only it seemed that Martin Kidd and Saw Hogan kind of got things sewed up like a sow's ear here at The Pirate's Den.

"Never thought of it that way. Bound to run into drovers who have sold their saddles or New York dudes who ain't too careful how they chew their grub."

At that moment Lance felt the presence of someone else. Someone behind his back. He turned and there was the Captain standing there, a thin cigar clenched between his teeth. His sidewinder eyes were more close-set than Lance had remembered. You almost expected a forked tongue to come slithering out from between his glistening lips.

"Well, well, Mr. Jordan. Why don't you come and join the rest of us. Sort of a wake for poor, unfortunate little Benny."

"Guess I thought too much of him to use him for an excuse to get liquored up," Lance said. Martin

Kidd's smile didn't waver. "Besides, I've got some work to do."

"Always a busy body," Kidd said, knowing exactly how that would play with Lance. Only he was wrong, it didn't.

"Wouldn't happen to know where your hired hand Saw Hogan is, would you?"

Kidd's eyes drew even narrower for just the briefest time. Then he recovered quickly. "Hogan isn't in my pocket. He just spends a lot of time here at The Den. His recreation, you might say."

Lance knew he had struck a nerve. "Then Mr. Hogan does spend some time in his own office, working for himself."

Kidd ground the cigar out in a canister of sand. "Cal, you'd better get back to work. As for you, Mr. Jordan, if you don't wish to join the rest of us, then I suggest you leave right away."

With that Cal began to sort the letters once more and Lance took his time walking across the hotel lobby to the front door. He caught the Captain's reflection in the gilt-edged mirror that was near the door and he was watching Lance's every move.

Outside, Lance walked the short distance to Saw Hogan's office. On the way he thought about the bushwacker of the other night. It hadn't been Marshal Crawley, because when he had seen him at the funeral he didn't appear to be wounded. To Lance that only left Wade Briley. He should have taken Kidd up on the invitation whether he intended to take a drink or not. At least he would have had an excuse to look around for Hap Briley.

Saw Hogan's business was just off Main Street. It was a small place with an office in the front and a larger room in the back where he stored the wooden caskets and prepared the bodies for burial.

Lance rapped on the front door and waited. He was still thinking about Hap Briley and also Uncle Ephraim. Could he be this McDeke person who had died at the hotel? Could this be just some loco mix-up and there really was someone by the name of Zeke McDeke staying in Jubilee? It seemed too far-fetched for Lance to believe.

Nobody came to the door so Lance rapped again, only louder. He waited. Still there was no answer. Lance peered through the plate glass window. He couldn't see any movement from within.

"You lookin' for Saw-Bones Hogan?" a man's voice came from behind.

Lance turned quicked around. He was face to face with Orie Tybolt.

"Oh, it's you, Lance," Orie said.

" 'lo, Orie. I wanted to do some jawin' with Hogan. Guess he ain't in his office."

Orie shook his head. "Saw him ride out of town right after the funeral."

Lance nodded. "Thanks, Orie. How come you ain't over with half the men at the Cutlass Room?"

"Take more'n a free drink to get me to ever cotton to that Martin Kidd. Never did like the man and him makin' generous all of a sudden don't sit right with me."

"That's the way I feel too," Lance said. "Never did hit it off with the man. Something about him I don't trust."

"Something! Everything about that scalawag I don't trust. He and that Saw Hogan is in cahoots. They got it all tied up with a neat, dirty ribbon."

"What are you talkin' about, Orie?"

"Shoot, everybody in town knows Saw Hogan writes them death certificates just the way Captain Kidd orders him to. No secret about that."

"Are you sure of that, Orie?"

Orie sniffed and scratched behind his ear. " 'course I'm sure. Just mosey over to Boot Hill. Lots of fresh graves over there. Almost every one of 'em spent their last days at The Den."

This was all news to Lance, but it didn't surprise him any. Nothing he heard about the Captain came as a surprise to Lance.

"Better be heading out," Orie said. "The missus is waiting for me over at the store."

"Would you do something for me, Orie?"

"Name it."

"Tell Harley I'll be along any minute. I got to do some checkin' at the cemetery."

Orie just nodded. "Do that. Take care, Lance. If I see Saw-Bones on the way out of town, I'll tell him you're lookin' for him."

Lance waited until Orie had gone before he tried

the door one more time. Satisfied that Orie had been right, he headed toward the cemetery.

When he got there he found that Benny's grave had been filled in and someone had placed some flowers around the headstone. But Lance hadn't come to the cemetery for that. He wanted to see if he could find any evidence of his uncle's burial.

Lance wandered among the headstones and wooden crosses. He felt a faint uneasiness as he passed by so many graves. They appeared fresh and no grass or weeds were growing over them.

He made a round of the graves but he didn't find what he was searching for. Uncle Ephraim, or Zeke McDeke, was nowhere to be found, although he saw several mounds of turned earth that were graves without any markings.

Lance decided he had been away from the store too long. Harley was a good boss but he didn't want to take advantage of his good nature.

It didn't take him long to get shuck off the cemetery. Once he was outside he paused for a minute to look back. Somewhere out there lay the remains of his uncle, he would find out where he was buried and how he died and what became of the money he was carrying.

At that moment shots rang out in town. There was loud shouting and swearing and more blasts from six-shooters. Lance's first thoughts were of Harley all alone at the store. He bolted toward town, racing along Piute Street until he got to Main Street.

Lance wasted no time in heading toward the store. He was relieved and out of breath when he saw Harley standing in the doorway of the store.

"You all right?"

"Fine as a crow's feather. Been worried about you. Orie said you were over to the cemetery."

"Had something to do over there. What's all the shootin' about?"

Harley pointed down the street, in the direction of the Red Gulley. "Coming from down there. From all the cussin' and caterwauling I'd say some drunken drovers was trying to lasso the town."

"At least you're safe," Lance said. "Maybe we'd better head inside in case there are any stray bullets lookin' for a target."

Harley looked as though he hadn't thought about that. "Good idea."

They moved out of the doorway just as the shooting began again. None too soon, a bullet pinged off the door and sent a shower of spinters into the dusty air.

"Dadburn, that's gettin' too close. I'm tempted to go down there and give 'em all a wherefore."

"You're going to stay right here. If anybody's going down to the Red Gulley it will be me."

"Then what you standin' here a jawin' for? Slap on that Colt and see what's happening."

Lance was tempted to do just that. Only he was torn between protecting Harley and getting caught up in a gunfight. Lance had never run from a fight in his entire life. Even in a town as small as San Anselmo there had been skirmishes and street fights.

Lance didn't have to do any deciding on his own. At that second a man poked his head inside the store and yelled, "Real trouble down at the Gully. Four drovers got the marshal pinned down. He could use another gun hand down there."

Lance grabbed his gun belt and slapped it around his waist and made sure his Colt .45 was loaded.

"Go find Saw Hogan," he yelled at the man. "We'll be needing him."

"Got you," the man said and sprinted away.

"Be careful," Harley said. "Marshal Crawley ain't much but he is all the law we got around Jubilee. And watch your back."

"I'll be careful. You stay inside."

Harley spit. "No need to remind me. I'm going to wait here with my shotgun. If one of them drovers staggers this far downtown he'll be able to see daylight out of his pickled gizzard."

Lance left the store by the back way. His plan was to come up behind the Red Gulley and maybe take the drovers by surprise. As he briskly moved down the alley he could hear an occasional shot being fired from in front of the saloon. Lance never thought he would be on Marshal Crawley's side, but he soothed his conscience by justifying what he was doing as being on the side of law and order.

The back of the Red Gulley was dead ahead. As Lance got nearer the voices of the men grew louder.

They were taunting the marshal with slurred, drunken voices.

"Come on out, Marshal. All we want to do is put a hole in that tin star of yours."

"Show us what a big man you are, Marshal. Maybe we'll just put our tails between our legs and high-tail it out of here."

Even though Lance held no great love for Marshal Crawley, he didn't like to hear any man being treated like that. It made his stomach tighten and the muscles sore in his shoulders.

Lance cautiously moved to the back door of the saloon. His plan was to go through the Red Gulley and see if he could surprise the drovers, however many there were. He stepped onto the wooden planks that led to the door and when he reached it, he slowly opened it and eased himself inside.

Lance found himself in the kitchen, or what passed for one. It was just a wood-burning stove and a sink with a wide counter space. The cook was doing something with a pot on the stove, but when he saw Lance with his Colt drawn he stepped back.

"No gun, I don't have no gun," he said lifting his hands in a submissive gesture.

"I'm not after you. I'm here to help the marshal."

"He's outside. Behind a barrel."

"How many men is he facing out there?"

The cook didn't hesitate. "Three was the way I heard it."

"Who all is in there?" Lance motioned with his head toward the bar.

"Just a couple of lowlives and the barkeep. There was a bunch of drovers but they left town. All but those three outside."

"You stay here."

"Wild buffaloes couldn't drag me out of my kitchen right now. No way they could."

With those final words, Lance went through the swinging doors into the bar. Even though there were a few men nursing their beers at the bar, it was quiet as if nobody was there. The barkeep was drying a glass with a towel and staring out the fly-specked plate glass window. He didn't see Lance until he was midway across the room.

"You one of them?" the barkeep asked.

Lance shook his head. "I'm standing with the marshal. Seein' if I can help."

"Wouldn't go out there if I was you, feller," one of the men said. "Too many against one."

"He's right," said another man. "Be another grave dug next to Benny's before sundown."

Lance ignored them. He wouldn't get any backing from those men. The barkeep, he wasn't so certain about. Never knew what kind of weapon a barkeep kept hidden below the apron of the bar.

"Just watch yourself," the barkeep said. "Two of them are across the street in front of Jake Homesteader's farrier shop. The other one is next door behind a hitched wagon."

"Thanks, that helps," Lance said and he walked over to the batwinged doors. At that moment, shots were fired and one pinged against the door jam splintering the wood.

The shots had come from across the street. They were followed quickly by a burst of gunfire from somewhere near the door. That had to be Marshal Crawley's response. From where he stood, Lance could see Crawley crouched behind a barrel that was beginning to look like it had been used for target practice.

Glancing across the street, Lance could see the two men the barkeep had told him about. They were standing in the shadows of the farrier's store front. Both of them were swaying slightly as they reloaded.

One of them called out, "Come on out, Marshal. You don't want us and the whole town to think you are chicken-livered, do you?"

Both men made the sound of a mother hen clucking to her chicks and then they burst into loud, mocking laughter. The sound echoed throughout the deserted street.

At that moment Crawley made the mistake of letting them get his goat. He showed himself, standing upright with his wide, expansive chest showing as he recklessly fired shots in the direction of the two drovers.

That was all the man waiting beside the wagon needed and his gun blast caught the marshal by surprise and Crawley let out a startled cry before ugly splotches of blood soaked his chest as he crumpled to the ground.

Lance quickly stepped out from the protection of the saloon and fanned the trigger on his Colt .45. He had sighted the gunman and the volley of bullets sped to their mark with such a force that the man spun around twice before dropping into the dry, dusty street.

It took Lance only a few seconds to reload as he sprinted to the barrel to see to Marshal Crawley. He had a feeling it was too late but Crawley was still breathing heavily as he knelt beside him.

"Playing the big hero," Crawley managed to get out. "Still don't like you," were what later Lance remembered were his final words.

Lance propped Crawley up against the barrel and peered out at the two men across the street. It had taken a little bit of time before what had happened penetrated the haze of alcohol. When they realized exactly what had happened, it made them angry. They carelessly stepped forward, out from the protection of the shadows. They fired blindly at where Lance and Crawley were hidden. Their bullets nicked and splattered the wood behind them, but didn't come a hair close to either Lance or the marshal.

Lance waited until they had emptied their sixguns. Then he stood up. He pointed his weapon dead center on the two advancing men.

"Drop 'em or you're both dead," he called out in a hard, level voice.

The two men fumbled with their cartridges to fill

the empty chambers but before they could finish the job the doors to the saloon were flung open. There stood the bartender with a shot gun aimed at them.

"Do what he said," the barkeep said angrily. "All I need is a reason to pull the trigger on this shotgun."

The two drovers dropped their guns. Even though they were still drunk from the afternoon's drinking bout, they were beginning to sober up. The heavy-looking shotgun and the lethal hand of the young scamp who had come to the aid of the marshal were enough to discourage them.

"Get a couple of men to take the marshal back to his office. I'm hauling these two into jail cells."

The barkeep acted quickly. He went inside the saloon and came back with two wide-eyed men prodded by the shotgun barrel. They got on either side of Marshal Crawley and picked him up and headed for the jailhouse.

Meanwhile, Lance covered the two drovers as he motioned for them to follow the men who were carrying Crawley's body. It was a slow procession down the street with the two drovers glancing every now and again over their shoulders at Lance who never wavered his hold on his Colt.

One by one townsfolk appeared on the street to watch the procession. Windows were lifted and doors slowly opened as the good citizens of Jubilee quietly viewed the body of Marshal Crawley being taken to the jailhouse.

Lance didn't know what he would do after the men

were incarcerated, but he hoped the marshal would recover from his wounds. He sometimes looked at the townspeople as they gathered in nervous little groups and saw something in their eyes that puzzled him. It was a though they all secretly were thinking the same thing . . . whatever that might be.

When they got to the jail, the barkeep opened the door for them.

"Better lay him down on this blanket," he said, taking one from a shelf and spreading it out on the floor.

"You two just keep on walking into those cells," Lance said, and he nudged one of the drovers with his Colt.

There were two cells and Lance put one man in each one. That way they wouldn't be tempted to cook up some scheme to break free of the jail.

Lance found the key ring and locked the doors to the cells. The two drovers sat down on the bunks holding their throbbing heads between the palms of their hands. They knew they were in big trouble and they couldn't remember for the life of them how all the fracas got started.

"How did this get started?" Lance asked the barkeep who was kneeling beside the marshal. The two drovers glanced over at the man who had bested them as if he had read their minds.

The barkeep slowly shook his head. "How does anything like this get started? Some drover boastin' and braggin'. I heard something about the backhand slip or throwin' the hoolihan. One drover said he was better'n another. Another drover denied that. By that time most of the other drovers had high-tailed it out of there."

It was a story Lance had heard before. The way most fights and shoot-outs got started. Mix a good braggart with some rotgut whiskey and someone to call his bluff and you got the makings of a fight.

The door was flung open and Saw Hogan stood there looking like he had been riding a whirlwind. His hair was standing on end and his coat was buttoned all wrong. He looked at Lance then the other men and lastly at Marshal Crawley sprawled on the floor.

"What's been going on here? Orie came riding out to where I was communing with nature hell bent for leather. He said something about a shoot out."

"Marshal got it," Lance said. "We brought him in here to get him off the street."

"Let's have a look," Hogan said and he pushed one of the men aside as he examined the marshal. It didn't take him long to pronounce Crawley dead.

"Better take him over to my place," he said to the men who had carried Crawley over. "Here's a key to the front door."

The men looked at each other, then one of them said, "Where'll we put him?"

"There's a table inside. That'll do nicely. Got to make him officially dead. Death certificate and all that."

The two men said nothing else. Together with the barkeep they left the office with the body of the marshal. When they had gone, Hogan asked Lance how it had happened. But Lance instead asked Hogan about his uncle. Hearing Hogan speak of the death certificate brought all of that back to Lance.

"You say he was staying at The Pirate's Den? What did he look like?"

Lance described Uncle Ephraim to Hogan who chewed on his lower lip for a few seconds and then a spark flared in his eyes. "Now I remember. Died in his sleep. Must have had a bad heart."

"His heart was as sound as a rock," Lance said. "He never had a sick day in his life."

Hogan looked suspiciously at Lance. "You must have known this McDeke fellow pretty well."

"That's right."

"Friend of yours?"

"No he wasn't."

"Relative, maybe?"

"Maybe is right. He was my uncle. Been looking for him for a long time now. Only I don't believe he died the way you said he did."

Hogan's lower lip jutted out like a fleshy turnip top. "You saying you are doubting my integrity?"

Lance didn't flinch or bat an eye. "I'm saying my uncle's heart wasn't what caused his death. Where is the death certificate?"

Hogan was getting edgy. This young upstart was asking too many questions. He was getting too close to learning a truth. A truth that only he and Martin

Kidd were privy to. "I got to be going. I've got a dead marshal over at my place who needs attending to."

"I want to see my uncle's death certificate."

Hogan moved toward the door sidestepping the bloody blanket that once held the body of the late marshal. "It's somewhere. . . . somewhere over at my office. Or it's in the Captain's office, I forget which."

"I want to see that certificate," Lance repeated with a steely edge to his voice that made Hogan more nervous than ever. He stammered and flushed a beet red and then managed to get out, "I'll find it for you. Don't get all riled up. I'll find it for you."

With that, Saw Hogan went outside where he took in some deep breaths before he headed for his office. He was worried, more worried than he had ever been in his life.

Chapter Eight

Even above the din of the men's voices Martin Kidd could hear his name being shouted. He turned from where he was standing at the bar as one of Hap Briley's men came through the batwinged doors. When the man saw Martin he cried out to him, "Marshal's been killed. There was a shootout over at the Red Gulley. Crawley got the worst end of it."

Those words cut through the noise of the townsmen who all turned to look at the newcomer.

"Who did it?" One of the townsmen asked angrily.

"Dunno. But I heard there was a bunch of drovers hootin' it up over at the Gulley. They been at it ever since the place opened."

"Where is the marshal?" came a question from another citizen.

"Hear he's been taken over to the hoosegow. That

feller what works at the mercantile store shot the man who killed Crawley. He's kinda taken over."

"You mean Lance Jordan?" another man said. "He's a good man."

"Must be good on the draw too," was an observation.

"We ought to go over there," a voice spoke firmly. "Sort of show our respect and support of that Jordan feller."

It seemed like a good idea and the men in a group left the Cutlass Room and an angry Martin Kidd for whom things weren't working out the way he wanted. Kidd stood with a rigid back against the bar while Rose tried to comfort him as she ran a hand along his arm. Kidd flung her hand away with such fury, Rose had to grasp the bar in order to not fall down.

"Save that for one of your paying customers," Kidd said in a scorning voice. "You," he called to the man who had brought the news of the marshal's death. "Follow those men and see what they're up to. Then come back here and fill me in."

The man took a quick swallow from a half-empty glass of whiskey left by one of the townsmen and shoved his Stetson low over his forehead before making tracks to follow the men.

Kidd walked past Rose without a word as he headed for his office. The barkeep tried to comfort Rose. "Don't pay him any mind, Rosie. He didn't know what he was doing."

"Go to hell," Rose said. "He knew damned well what he was doin'. And don't call me Rosie."

Rose didn't stay for a drink. She headed for her room in a small bungalow behind the hotel to repair the rip in her dress and let her anger cool down.

At the jail, Lance was talking to Gil Ivory who was about Lance's age and unmarried too. His father owned a small spread about a few miles from Jubilee. Gil always wanted to be a lawman, in fact, he had practiced quick-drawing for over a couple of years. He had no hankering to be marshal, but he wouldn't turn down the opportunity to be deputized.

"What's going to happen now, Lance?" Gil asked, side-stepping the blanket that Lance hadn't bothered to remove.

"I dunno. Guess I'll just have to wait and see what the folks here decide to do about Crawley. They'll have to find somebody to take his place."

Gil tried not to show too much interest in what had happened to Marshal Crawley for fear of being thought of as nosey. Still, he had a natural curiosity.

"How did he get it? I mean, where was he when he took the bullet?"

"Front of the Red Gulley. This bunch of rowdy drovers had him pinned down behind a barrel. I got the one that hit him."

"Where's he now?"

"Probably being toted away to Saw Hogan's. The barkeep probably wants to clear out any reminders of what happened over there. Bad for business, you know," Lance's mouth smiled in a twisted way. He had to watch himself or he might become jerky-hard. Couldn't go back to San Anselmo with that kind of change. Might not sit too well with his Susan.

"Looks like we got company coming," Gil said as he leaned over to peer out the window.

Lance had already heard the sound of voices as he and Gil had been talking. He stepped over to the door as the voices grew louder to see what all the ruckus was about. Lance opened the door and walked casually outside. Gil was right behind him.

The men gathered around Lance as they neared the jail-house. They had questions to ask.

"Is it true Crawley got shot?"

"True. He's over at Hogan's right now."

"What about the drover what done it?"

"He's over at Hogan's too."

"You finished him off?"

"Had to."

A kind of low but meaningful cheer went up from the crowd.

"Hear tell there was three of them. Where's the other two?"

"Inside. I got 'em locked up."

"They gonna be tried?"

"For drunk and disorderly I'd reckon. Didn't really do much damage. Only I got 'em locked up until they sober up."

"We'll need a new marshal."

"That's the God's truth. I think we got a good candidate standing right here."

Lance looked at Gil. Gil stepped back and shook his head. "They don't mean me. It's you that they're speaking at."

Lance quickly turned to face the mob that was conferring.

"I gotta get back to work. Mr. Denker'll be wondering what happened to me."

"Hold on, Lance," came a familiar voice. It was Harley Denker who had joined the crowd. "I think you ought to at least listen to what these men have to say."

Harley elbowed his way through the throng and stood beside Lance. Lance whispered to him. "I don't like the looks of this. We ought to get back to the store. No tellin' what a mob will do once they get riled."

Harley looked at the crowd and whispered back. "This ain't no mob. They are just concerned citizens. I think they got you pegged."

"For what?"

"Marshal, that's what."

"Not me. I finish what I came to Jubilee for and then I am riding back to San Anselmo."

"Never thought of you as being a quitter."

That got Lance's back up. "Who says I'm a quitter?"

"Nobody yet. Just wanted you to know what folks might get into their heads."

Lance didn't like what Harley was saying. He didn't

think he liked the whole idea of his being marshal. But he had more or less asked for it when he stuck his chin into what wasn't his fight.

"So what you say, Jordan?" a man asked in a loud, booming voice. "You takin' the job?"

"We need to vote on it," some civic-minded person put in.

"That's right, let's do this thing legal like," the first man said. "All in favor of electing Lance Jordan our new marshal say aye!"

The ayes had it, not a single man cried nay. "Looks like you've been elected, Marshal," Harley said and he patted Lance on the back.

"Now wait just a darn minute." Lance said facing the crowd with a determined look. "It ain't that I don't appreciate what you think of me. I only got to make something clear right off the start."

Nobody said a word. They just stood there listening to what Lance had to say. He could see the looks on the faces of the men. Not one of them toted a frown. They all had a faint, proud smile on their lips.

Lance cleared his throat. "I'll accept the job on one condition."

"Name it," a voice spoke from the crowd.

"That I take it if I can appoint Gil as a deputy. And if I don't work out, you find yourself another man. I hadn't planned on stayin' in Jubilee too long. I got myself a gal over in New Mexico I aim to marry."

There was laughter from the men. "You can take time off for that," another man said. "Jubilee's a right good place for a family man. After all you done got a deputy to run things while you're tying the knot."

Harley had left his side and gone into the marshal's office. He came out with two tin stars in his hand. Without a word he pinned one star on Lance's vest.

"I now officially appoint you marshal of Jubilee, Pima County, Arizona."

Harley then handed the other star to Lance. Lance held the star in the palm of his hand for a moment and saw a flash of sunlight burst out with a quick, sudden spark.

Lance moved to where Gil was standing. "Didn't bother to ask you, Gil. Maybe you ain't interested in being deputized."

"If you don't give me the star, I'll take it away from you," Gil said, taking a stand with his legs spread wide apart and his hands resting on his holsters.

Lance pinned the star on Gil then shook his hand. "Don't know what the official words are but as far as I'm concerned you are now my deputy."

A cheer went up from the crowd and the men came forward to congratulate Lance and his new deputy. There was a lot of back slapping and hand shaking and then the men went away in groups back to their work or families. A block from the jailhouse, the man Kidd had sent to spy on the proceedings hung out in the shadows not wanting to be seen by any of the men.

Determining what had happened by the cheering, he pushed his Stetson forward on his head and slunk away back to The Pirate's Den. He dreaded going there because more than once he had felt the wrath of The Captain when he was angry about something he couldn't control or things hadn't gone his way. But he went anyway.

Martin Kidd was at a gaming table slowly letting chips trickle from one hand to the other. When the man told him what he had seen Kidd slammed the chips down on the table with such force the drinks that were there fell with a crashing shatter to the floor.

"Clean this mess up," Kidd yelled at the barkeep. To the man who had brought the news of Jordan's becoming the new marshal he said, "Go get Briley. Tell him I want to see him . . . right now!"

The man skittered away not waiting for Kidd to say anything more. Kidd leaned back in his chair and stared at the ceiling with a look of utter anger in his eyes.

After the men had drifted away, Lance and Harley were left alone with Gil Ivory.

"What about my job?" Lance said.

"You got a job. You're the new town marshal."

"I know that. I mean my job at the store. You need someone to help out."

"I'll get by. There's always some drifter coming through town who needs a few dollars for some beans," he said with a wink.

Leaving Harley's employment wasn't the easiest thing Lance had ever done. Harley had been good to him, offered him a job when he knew nothing about him. Besides, Harley was getting too old to do all the heavy lifting that went along with running the store.

"I dunno. Maybe I could handle both jobs."

Harley just shook his head. "You are the town marshal and that's that. You'll have your hands full just trying to keep peace at the Red Gulley and The Pirate's Den. Besides, I think I can talk Reuben Mundy into helping out. He could use the money."

It had been a long time since Lance had seen Reuben Mundy. He had wondered what had happened to him. Maybe he would work out for Harley, maybe not. Lance would keep an eye on Mundy to make sure he treated Harley right.

"How about our prisoners?" Gil asked as he ran a denim sleeve across the face of the badge pinned to his shirt.

"We watch them. When they sober up I'll check with the judge over in Tucson to see what we ought to do with them."

"Sounds like a good idea, Marshal," Gil said. "I'll go inside to watch over them."

"Be right there," Lance said. He wanted a little time alone with Harley and he wasn't certain what to say.

"Best be gettin' over to Mundy's shebang to see if he's interested in workin' for an honest day's wage."

"You sure you want Mundy workin' for you, Mr. Denker?"

"Don't worry. I'll watch him like a hawk watches a kangaroo rat. Mundy was once a good worker, when he had his spread. Just got the gamblin' fever and lost everythin' in this world to Martin Kidd."

Lance had heard the story many times. How Mundy was once a pretty well-to-do rancher. Then how he had taken a big fall. He had gambled at The Den for high stakes with Kidd himself and had lost. Even though Mundy had swallowed his pride and begged Kidd for some show of mercy because of his wife and children, Kidd had told him he ran a business. "It's not good business sense to let feelings interfere," was the way he put it.

Shamed and penniless, Mundy had had to give up his prosperous ranch and move his family to what passed for a house on the outskirts of Jubilee. It was a humiliating experience for someone as proud and full of self-importance as Reuben Mundy had been. He had never forgotten what Kidd had done, even though it was Mundy himself who actually was at fault.

"Someday I'll get even with that four flusher," Lance had on more than one occasion heard Mundy mouth those words. "A man like that don't deserve to live."

Lance had dismissed what he had heard since Reuben Munday's threadbare appearance gave not indication of his once healthy prosperity.

"Just let me know, Harley," Lance said, dropping the Mister Denker. "If he tries to hornswoggle you. I'll toss him in the hoosegow. Family man or not."

Harley said that he would do just that. Then he

shook Lance's hand one final time and hobbled away in the direction of the Mundy place.

Lance watched Harley leave and felt sorry for the old man. He hoped Harley would be able to find an honest, hard worker. If Mundy didn't work out, he would personally find someone to help him.

Going back inside, he found Gil standing on the outside of the cells. The two drovers had fallen asleep and were snoring so loud it would wake the residents on Boot Hill.

Gil walked over to the coffee pot that was still warm. "Want a cup?" Gil said, lifting the pot into the air.

"Not right now. How are our prisoners doing?"

"Sleepin' like they didn't have a worry in the world. Want me to get 'em up?"

"Let 'em be, Gil. They'll have enough trouble on their hands when they get over their drunken snoozin'."

Gil poured a cup of coffee and sat down in a chair near the cells.

Lance went over to Marshal Crawley's desk and opened a few of the drawers. He didn't find much in the way of personal effects. There was a small packet of tobacco and some rolling paper, a box of matches, and a dog-eared copy of a Sears catalogue. Thumbing through the catalogue, Lance came to a photograph of a woman whom he figured must have been Crawley's late wife.

"Not much to show for a man's life," Lance said,

putting everything on the desk top. "Ever hear if Crawley had any living kinfolk?"

Gil shook his head. "Just know he was from Wyoming before he landed in Jubilee. The only folks he ever cottoned to were the Abbotts. Even then he wasn't all that close, from what I hear."

"The Abbotts? Maybe I'll ride over there with these things. See if Crawley had any living relations."

Lance found a sack to put Crawley's belonging in and then said to Gil. "Mind takin' over while I ride out to the Abbott place?"

"You're the boss," Gil said with a grin. "Don't mind ridin' shotgun. Just don't let those townsfolk decide they want to promote me."

Lance had long ago learned that Gil wasn't a leader. He was easy-going, almost to the point of being lazy. He was reliable and never one to quickly rile. Lance knew Gil was honest along with being dependable. He felt lucky he had found a friend like Gil Ivory.

"Be back soon as I can."

"Don't rush. I reckon our prisoners ain't going to be up in the saddle for a long time yet."

Lance had to walk back to the store for his horse. He noticed the front door had a closed sign on it. Harley was still probably over jawin' with Reuben Mundy.

Lance saddled up his gelding and headed out of town. As he passed The Pirate's Den, he saw Martin Kidd leaning on the batwinged doors staring at him as he passed by. As a courtesy, Lance touched the brim of his hat which made the Captain quickly turn his head and look in another direction.

Seeing the Captain once again reminded Lance of why he had come to Jubilee. After learning of Uncle Ephraim's death at the hotel it didn't take Lance long to put two and two together. He felt that it was a racket Kidd and Saw Hogan were in together. If a person had a sizable amount of money with him and his departure might not be missed, he would be quickly disposed of at the hotel. With Saw Hogan writing a trumped-up death certificate, it was a nice little profitable game Captain Kidd was running.

Lance felt that what he should do would be to shuck the badge and the marshal's job, find the missing money, and head back to San Anselmo. That was what he had come to town for. Only Lance knew it wouldn't be that easy. He had accepted the job and when he felt Gil was responsible enough he would leave town.

Being a marshal might, after all, have its advantages. Especially in tracking down Uncle Ephraim's grave and then finding the money, if there was any left.

Lance saw the Abbott place ahead and put Uncle Ephraim and the missing money out of his thoughts.

Tom was in the corral doing some repair work, but he stopped when he saw Lance and leaped over the corral fence.

Lance slipped out of the saddle and told Tom what had been going on in town. Harriett came out to join them and she cried when she learned that the marshal had died from his wounds.

"We'll take care of his belongings," Harriett said. "He didn't have any relatives that I know of, but we'll store his possessions here just in case someone calls for them."

Lance stayed for a cup of coffee and to tell them in more detail what had happened. After about an hour he said, "I'd better get back to town. Gil's a good man, but I don't want to leave him alone too long."

"You'll make a good marshal," Tom encouraged. "Just what Jubilee needs."

"I dunno. We'll see what happens down the line," Lance said. "You know I got a gal over in New Mexico. Susan and I are planning a wedding. We were, that is, until all this with Uncle Ephraim came up."

Tom put an arm around Harriett. "You can still get married up. Just take some time off and bring your bride back to Jubilee."

"What a grand idea," Harriett said. "You know a house goes with the job of marshaling."

Lance thought about what the Abbotts had said as he left their place. He hadn't thought that far ahead. But what they had said made sense. He liked Jubilee and wouldn't mind settling down here. Lance thought he knew Susan well enough that she just might take a liking to living in Jubilee too.

It was at this point that Lance saw the rider not too far down the trail from him. At first he wasn't certain, so he spurred his gelding into a faster trot. The nearer he got the more positive he became.

The rider was staring straight ahead and not paying

any attention to being followed. The horse he was riding was a piebold. Uncle Ephraim's piebold. Now that he was closer, Lance was positive. And this close he recognized the rider. It was Hap Briley.

Chapter Nine

"Yo! Briley!" Lance called out.

Briley heard his name and turned his head to see who had hailed him. When he saw Lance he spurred his mustang into a frantic, fast gallop. The tables had been turned on Briley, or so he thought. He was now being the one pursued. All he could think of was to get to Jubilee as fast as possible.

Cort Danley had found him under orders from the Captain. All he had said was, "Kidd wants to see you . . . now!" It was enough to fling Hap into his saddle and head for Jubilee. Whatever it was must be important. Now with Jordan after him he felt there might be some connection.

Lance wasn't surprised when Briley hightailed and goaded his horse to move. It was what he expected from the back-shooting low life. Now that he had seen

Uncle Ephraim's piebold, he felt that Briley had something to do with his murder. Yes, pure and simple, Uncle Ephraim must have been murdered. He didn't suffer a heart attack and he probably didn't go without a struggle. Unless he was in such a condition that he couldn't put up a fight.

Briley was taking a wide lead now. The piebold was a runner, faster than Lance's gelding. Briley was headed for Jubilee. Probably on his way to see Martin Kidd. A lot of men were on Kidd's payroll. The bunch of drovers who had shot holes in the sky over at the schoolhouse the day Lance arrived in Jubilee were Briley's boys.

Lance wanted to talk to Briley, if that was at all possible, about his part in what had happened to Uncle Ephraim. He also wanted to know what had become of the money Uncle Ephraim had stolen.

Ahead of them loomed Jubilee. Today a fine wind keened across the open desert and flung tiny pellets of sand and grit kicked up by the piebold into Lance's face. He had to raise the kerchief tied around his neck to keep the sand out of his mouth and nose.

Because of the sudden burst of sand carried on the wind, Lance temporarily lost sight of Briley when they got into Jubilee.

Lance slowed his gelding to a trot as he glanced around when he moved down Main Street.

"Ho, there, Marshal Jordan!" a man called as he came out of the shadow of a porch. It was Orie Tybolt.

"Afternoon, Orie. Word travels faster 'n a bobcat with a burr under his tail."

Orie chuckled. "Me and the missus are right glad you got the job. Want you to know the whole town is backin' you."

Lance offered his thanks, then asked, "Did you happen to see Hap Briley come past here? Been lookin' for him."

"Hap Briley," Orie said disgustedly. "Hope you want to toss him and that gang of his in jail and throw the key away."

"Maybe it will turn into that," was all that Lance would confide in Orie.

"Well, in that case, he did come a skeddadling down this way. Almost ran me over he was in such a gol-dang hurry."

That was what Lance needed to know. "Thanks, Orie. Would like to stay and jaw with you, but I'm in kind of a hurry."

"Understand. Far be it from me to stand in the way of the law being carried out."

Orie stood aside and Lance continued on down Main Street. Knowing Hap Briley as little as he wanted to, Briley would probably be on his way to The Den. When he caught up with the man he had better have a bill of sale on the piebold or Lance would slap him in jail as quickly as he could for horse stealing.

Arriving at The Den, Lance reined in his gelding and leaned forward in the saddle. There were a few horses tied to the hitchrail, but not one of them was Uncle Ephraim's piebold. Lance wondered if he could have figured Briley wrong. Maybe he didn't come directly to see Martin Kidd. If not, then where else had he got to? As far as Lance knew, Briley didn't have any friends outside of The Pirate's Den. If you chose to call Captain Martin Kidd a friend.

Then Lance thought there must be a rear entrance to The Den. There had to be and that would have been where Briley would have left his horse. Even if he didn't know that the new marshal was after him.

Lance started to ride around to the alley behind The Den when he heard Gil Ivory call out his name.

"Lance . . . Marshal Jordan!" Gil shouted as he ran across the dusty street from the jailhouse to The Den. It sounded peculiar to Lance to hear Gil call him Marshal, but he had to get used to it.

"What is it, Gil?"

"There's some shootin' going on over at The Red Gulley."

"Again? What's going on over there?"

"One of the regulars come over to the jailhouse and said to come a runnin'. Some drover friends of the three we got penned up are lookin' for trouble."

Lance had to make a quick decision. He figured Hap Briley would have to wait for a spell, the shoot-out over at The Gulley was something that wouldn't wait.

"I'll tie up my horse and be right with you," Lance said, quickly lowering himself to the ground. "We'll go over together and see what we can do about this."

Gil waited with his hands nervously fingering the hard, hand-carved butts of his six-shooter. Lance slipped his Winchester out of its scabbard and checked the chamber to see if it was loaded. Then he loaded an extra bean into his revolver so all the chambers were full.

"Ready," Lance finally said, and Gil solemnly nodded. Side by side they walked down the boardwalk, keeping as much in the shadows as possible so as to make themselves less of a target.

They hadn't gone but a block when they heard some loud, boisterous shouts and then the crackle of gunfire. Acting out of instinct, the two men slapped their holsters and brought out their weapons. Lance had his Winchester cradled in his left arm so he was free to hoist the six-shooter with his right hand.

"You nervous? I sure as heck am," Gil said in a raw, raspy voice.

"Try not to think about it," Lance cautioned, knowing how that must sound to Gil. "But, yeah, I am."

A second burst of yelling and gunfire came from The Gulley and a man ran past them holding onto his Stetson with both hands. Over his shoulder he cried, "Bunch of locos in there. Shootin' for no good reason at all. This town is going to the devil."

Having said that, the man leaped over the hitchrail and kicked up a plume of dust as he skedaddled for the safety of a building.

Lance and Gil were now close to the saloon. It was on the same side of the street with themselves. Overhead the sun was moving to the west and it gave them good, ample shade. The street was empty by this time and the drifting wind sent tiny whirlwinds spiraling into the dry, blue air. The only sounds came from within the saloon.

Lance was nervous and thinking quickly about the best way to handle these men. Their horses were tethered outside The Gulley. They seemed spooky and ready to bolt and run away at the slightest sound.

Lance whispered to Gil, "I'll make a run for the other side of the door and when I give you the sign, we'll rush 'em."

"Got it," Gil answered. He quickly checked the two Colt .45s in his hands. He was surprised how steady his hands were even though he was itching to get inside and see what was going on in there.

Lance's hands were steady too, only he was thinking he would be glad when this was all over. For a moment, a picture of Susan Wells flashed before his eyes. He couldn't figure out why he was thinking about her at a time like this.

The sound of the voices inside had died down somewhat. Lance figured he and Gil would wait until the drovers started in again. They would be distracted in their carryin' on and wouldn't be expecting him and Gil to come into the saloon.

They didn't have long to wait. There was a sudden yelp and an ear-splitting laugh followed by a volley of echoing shots.

Lance nodded to Gil and together they burst through the batwinged doors into the saloon.

There were three men standing at the bar, their guns raised over their heads. What customers there were in the saloon were all crouched for protection under tables and the barkeep was standing helpless at the edge of the bar, not able to get to his shotgun.

"Drop 'em . . . right now!" Lance shouted and the three men switched their attention from their gunfire to the two strangers who had entered the saloon.

Lance hadn't noticed a fourth drover who was across the room until a shot rang out. It whined past Lance's head and cracked a glass resting on a table across the room.

"Hit cover!" Lance yelled at Gil who already had overturned a table and motioned for Lance to come on over.

Lance leaped for cover and then fired off a few rounds at the drover across the room. There was no contest between a sober marshal and a drover who had been drinking hard liquor all morning. The shooter dropped to the floor and crawled all fours to the safety of a cabinet that had gotten tipped over sometime that afternoon.

The three men standing at the bar quickly realized what was happening and moved with lightning swiftness to take cover.

Gil had followed their movement with a trail of bullets that chipped the wooden floor sending sharp splinters flying in all directions. The stale air in the saloon was almost suffocating with the smell of gunpowder and smoke.

Not far from Lance, two regulars made a quick, frantic dash for the doors and their exit was punctuated by blasts from the three drovers near the bar. They were at the point of excitement and drunkenness that they would shoot at anything that moved.

To protect the regulars, Lance sent a barrage of bullets toward the three crouching drovers. He had no intention of hitting them, just to pin them down until he could figure out the best way to handle the situation.

Gil kept his eye on the fourth drover who had remained quiet all this time. He was still there because Gil could see the outline of his body in the dim light cast by the overhead lanterns.

One of the three drovers hiding beside the bar suddenly leaned over the table and fired a volley of shots at Lance and Gil; chips of wood spit out by the bullets dug into Lance's forehead and Gil yelped as one of them dug its way into his right cheek.

By this time the room was as smoky as a runaway prairie fire. Lance thought he heard footsteps and debated risking a look around the overturned table. When he did he saw the barkeep coming from behind the bar with his shotgun held steadily in his hands.

"They're gone!" he shouted. "Vamoosed out the back door."

It took a few seconds for the impact of what the

barkeep had said to sink in. Then Lance got to his feet with Gil struggling to rise beside him.

"Which way?" Lance called out.

The barkeep pointed his shotgun in the direction of the back door and followed Lance and Gil as they gingered their way through the maze of overturned tables and broken chairs to get to the back door.

By the time they saw daylight, they heard the sound of hoofbeats.

"They're gettin' away!" cried the barkeep. "Damn! Look what they done to the place."

"Know who they are?" Lance asked. "Or what outfit they're hitched to?"

The barkeep shook his head. "First I figured they was with those two you got hunkered down in the hoosegow. But they was just passin' on something they had heard on the trail."

"Don't reckon they'll be headed back this way any time soon," Gil said holstering his two six-guns.

"Better not. They rung up a pretty fair-sized bar bill. Not to mention the damage they done to the table and chairs. Either they'll pay or I'll be needing your services real bad, Marshal."

Lance just nodded. He couldn't think that far ahead. Right now he only took things one day at a time.

"Let me and Gil give you a hand at setting up these tables again."

"Oh, you don't have to do that, Marshal. 'Though I appreciate the offer."

In the end the barkeep took Lance up on the offer

and he and Gil spent a good half-hour righting the tables and putting what chairs were still useable back in position. By the time they finished, the Red Gulley had all the appearances of being open for business again.

The barkeep couldn't thank them enough. "Anytime you want to have a free drink or get something to eat, it's on the house."

"Appreciate that," Lance said. "Gil and I had better be going back to the jailhouse. See how our prisoners are doin'."

Before they left, the barkeep gave them some sandwiches and hard-boiled eggs to take along with them.

As they left the saloon, Gil cracked one of the eggs and took a bite off the top. "You reckon those men are gone for good? Or do you think they'll be back?"

"Hard to tell, but I kinda think they'll make a wide trail around Jubilee in the future."

Not far from the saloon, a man and his wife approached them. The man touched the brim of his hat and said, "Want to thank you, Marshal, for coming to help the bartender. Me and the missus don't think much of The Red Gulley, but we want to thank you anyway for what you and Gil done."

"It's our job," Lance said evenly.

"Other marshal wouldn't have done it," the woman said. "Hear he got shot. Really sorry about that. Don't take to shootin', no matter who gets shot. How is he doin'?"

Lance looked directly at the woman. She was plain-faced, sensible, and not bitter like a lot of folks he had met along the way to Jubilee. This was another reason he desired to try and talk Susan into coming to Jubilee and settling down.

"He died, ma'am," Lance said simply.

"Oh, I'm sorry," the woman answered. "We just heard there was the new marshal, we didn't know how come. We wish you all the best in the world, Marshal."

"And we're behind you and your deputy all the way," the husband added, then they walked quickly away.

"At least we got a lot of people backing us," Gil said, as they continued their walk to the jailhouse.

Along the way, as was the custom of a small town, people waved to Lance and Gil and said words of encouragement. It was heady words for Gil who squared his shoulders and got a slight swagger to his walk. Lance just shook his head when he saw how his young deputy was taking all this attention.

When they got to the jail, they found Tom Abbott there waiting for them.

"Just heard about the shoot-out. Anybody hurt?" he asked as Lance and Gil met up with him.

"Four drovers trying to rope the town," Lance said. "More hootin' than anything else. They're halfway to Tucson by now. What brings you to town, Tom?"

"Harriett needed something from Denker's and I said I'd make the ride. While I was here I thought I'd just see how you and Gil was doin'."

They talked for a while, then Tom got on his horse and told Lance to drop over before riding away.

After that, they went inside to check on the two drovers who were still out of the roundup.

"Looks like it's quiet here," Lance said. "You think you can handle things for about an hour? I got some business I got to take care of over at The Pirate's Den."

Gil said he could and didn't question why Lance would want to hang out over at The Captain's, he just accepted it.

Lance took a final look at the prisoners, then walked out of the office leaving Gil eating a sandwich and drinking day-old coffee.

On the way to The Den, Lance kept thinking about Uncle Ephraim's piebold and how it came to be in the possession of Hap Briley. By now he was fully convinced that Martin Kidd, Saw Hogan, and Briley all had a hand in his uncle's death.

He could see The Den ahead and there were a few horses tethered at the hitchrail. No piebold. Briley wouldn't be that stupid as to tie it up in plain sight. He probably had the horse hidden out behind The Den. To make certain he was right, Lance turned this side of The Den and sauntered down the boardwalk to the alley. He stopped just as the building met the alley. He was right, there was Uncle Ephraim's piebold tied behind the building.

Lance turned around and went back to the entry of The Den. He walked inside and once again was struck by the splendor of this hotel. He nodded to Cal Gordon who glanced at him while he was registering a guest.

He moved easily across the carpet and headed toward The Cutlass Room. He was sure that this was where he would find Briley.

He pushed open the batwinged doors and looked around easily. There were just a handful of customers in the room. He saw Rose Sparks as she came into the room from the other entry. She looked different to Lance, like she was nervous and she kept fiddling with her hair until she found a table with a tall, bearded cowhand who seemed really pleased to have her for company.

Hap Briley wasn't in the bar. Lance went over and spoke to the barkeep.

"Seen Briley today?"

The barkeep swiped at the mahogany bar with a damp cloth. "Hasn't been here. You need him?"

"Let's just say I'd like to speak to him. Got some explaining to do."

"Might be in Kidd's office. He hangs out in there a lot."

"Where's the office?"

"Just through that back entrance. You can't miss it. Real fancy piece of woodwork. Had it shipped in special from Mexico."

Lance nodded his thanks and started across the room toward the back entrance. He got stopped midway by a customer who he thought he recognized from The Red Gulley.

"Fine job you did a roustin' them drovers over at the Gulley," he sputtered. "Can I buy you a drink, Marshal? Sort of a thank you for what you done for me. Ain't every day somebody sticks up for Ole Gorey."

"Maybe next time, Gorey," Lance said. "Right now I got some work to do."

"Suit yourself," Gorey said, a little disappointed. "I owe you one, Marshal."

With that said, the man staggered back to the bar and nearly missed the stool as he sat down.

Lance went out the back entrance and came to the door that had to belong to Captain Martin Kidd. It was hand-carved and was a little too fancy for this part of the hotel.

Lance banged on the door and was taken back when it opened on its own.

"Kidd? Martin Kidd? It's Marshal Jordan," he said as he waited for Kidd to say something. No words were spoken so Lance pushed the door all the way open, his free hand resting on the butt of his Colt .45.

There was good reason why Martin Kidd didn't answer. He was in his office, all right. But he wouldn't ever speak another word. He lay on the floor on his back, his head had been smashed in and there was a pool of blood beneath it.

Chapter Ten

Lance stood looking down at the body of Martin Kidd with disbelief. Somehow he never thought that would be the end for the Captain. Behind the paper-scattered desk, the small safe stood wide open. From where Lance was standing, it looked as though some-one had started to clean it out and got interrupted by Martin Kidd.

If this was the way it happened, then Kidd must have come in and found the killer at work on the safe. There was a struggle and the Captain was hit over the head.

Lance finally moved from the doorway. He knelt down by the Captain's body and felt for life signs in case Kidd might still be alive. There was no pulse and Kidd wasn't breathing.

Standing upright, Lance gazed around the room and

saw an open window. He stepped over the body of the Captain and walked over to look out. The window faced an alley and Lance saw something glitter from a stray shaft of sunlight. It was a blood-stained poker. A poker that must have belonged to Kidd. Later Lance was to learn that it was the Captain's "good luck" piece he had brought with him all the way from Alaska.

It was just a short drop from the window to the alley below and Lance climbed down and retrieved the poker. He could see the traces of blood on the deadly end of the piece of iron.

"What's you got that for, Marshal?" a voice came out of nowhere. Lance turned his attention on the man who had offered him a drink earlier in the bar. The man was leaning against the side of the building, probably had taken a short cut through the alley on his way home.

"Come here," Lance said. The man straightened up by the sharp tone in Lance's voice. He swayed over to Lance. He smelled heavily of John Barleycorn and a winning battle against soap and water.

"I want you to go over to the jailhouse and tell my deputy to get his butt over here right now. You can handle that?"

The man belched and stood as straight as he was capable of doing in his condition. "Yes, I can handle that."

"Then skedaddle. I need Gil right now."

The man hurried away. Lance went back inside

Kidd's office through the open window. He took another look around to make sure his conclusions on how Captain Martin Kidd had come to his end were true. The open safe, the papers scattered all over the desk, the blood-stained poker—it couldn't have been anything but a robbery attempt that had turned deadly. And yet Lance felt that it just wasn't right. He didn't know why, just a feeling he had.

It wasn't long before Gil showed up. He pushed his hat back on his head when he walked into the room and saw the body of Martin Kidd.

"Who done him in, Lance? Was it a robbery?"

"Looks kinda that way. I want you to stay here and not let anyone in. I'm going to send someone for Saw Hogan. He's the best we got in the way of a coroner. Anyway he's available, that's what counts."

"I'll be right here. Nobody'll get past me."

"I'm relyin' on you, Gil."

He knew Gil was dependable, only it didn't hurt to stress a point. Gil leaned against the door jam with his hat still shoved forward on his head and his strong, heavy-muscled arms were folded across his chest.

Lance went down the narrow hallway to the door that opened into the Cutlass Room. A man came through the door at the same moment headed for someplace to relieve himself.

"Howdy, Marshal," he said in a slightly thick-crusted voice. "Somepin big goin' on down here?"

"That's right," Lance said. "Need some help, real bad."

The man was all attention. His eyes were focused on the tin badge that stood out like a light in a mine shaft.

"Anything I can do to help? Be glad to do anything I can."

"I need someone to fetch Saw Hogan. You know where Hogan's place is?"

The man nodded. "Been past it a few times. So far I haven't had no opportunity to go inside."

"Would you go over there pronto and tell Hogan he's got some business over at The Den?"

The cowboy lost the urge or forgot why he had ambled down the hallway.

"Sure thing. Sounds like you need him real bad."

"I do."

That was all the cowboy needed and he turned and high-tailed it out of the hallway, back into the Cutlass Room where he headed for Saw Hogan's office.

Lance followed the cowboy into the bar. When he got inside, he walked over to the bar.

"Don't want anyone goin' back there," Lance said to the barkeep after he had motioned him over.

"Trouble?"

"Big kind."

"Something happen to the Captain?"

"How did you know?"

The barkeep's face was a stone slab. You couldn't tell what he was thinking.

"Just a feelin', I guess. Is he dead?"

"That's right. Only keep it to yourself for the time being."

"You won't hear a word out of me."

Lance looked around at the patrons left in the Cutlass Room. There were about seven men scattered at different tables. The lone woman, Rose Sparks, was still talking to the tall, bearded cowboy.

Lance figured it wasn't anyone here or they would have long since made themselves scarce. The killer must have dropped the poker after he had climbed out the window and made a bee-line down the alley. No, it wasn't anyone in the bar, Lance felt pretty certain of that.

Rose got up from the table and shaking off the hand of the cowboy came over to where Lance was standing.

"Give the marshal a beer, Georgie," Rose said as she leaned against the bar.

Lance lifted his hand. "Not today, Rose. Got other things to do here."

Rose shrugged. "Just tryin' to be friendly. Most folks come into a saloon for a little pleasure. You different from most folks, Marshal? Maybe think yourself a little better?"

Lance didn't answer, he was looking at Rose whose hair was still unkept and her face was flushed, not from drinking, but for some other reason.

"Maybe some other time, Rose," Lance said and Rose ran a quick hand over her wayward locks trying to get some sort of order in them. Again, looking at her, Lance knew something was missing but he couldn't figure out what it was. Probably wasn't all that important anyway.

"I'll be here when you change your mind," Rose said, giving up on her hair. "Come around to my place any time you feel like it."

Lance had heard that Rose had her own small place behind The Den. Only those folks came to see her by personal invite. To Lance there was no temptation. Rose might be what some men wanted, but those men didn't have a girl like Susan waiting for them back in San Anselmo.

Again there was nothing for Lance to say to Rose. Maybe not about the obvious invitation, but he did have other questions he was looking for answers to.

"Anybody in here threaten Martin Kidd's life today?" he asked, and Rose shook her head.

"Don't think so today. Can't say that much for other times."

"What you sayin'? He was threatened?"

"Honey, if you were in his shoes, don't you think you might walk on somebody's toes?"

"Might."

"Well, there are plenty of men who weren't all that loco about the Captain."

"Name a few."

Rose reached for the drink Georgie had adoringly set on on the polished bar for her. Georgie would do anything for Rose; he would do just about anything, even kill for his little Rosie.

"Why ask me? I ain't goin' to start namin' names. Just take my word for it."

"You want a name, Marshal?" Georgie said, slinging the bar rag over his shoulder. "I'll give you one."

Lance turned to face the barkeep. Georgie wasn't above breaking the law, Lance knew this from the stories he had heard while working for Harley Denker. Many a man would sit for hours jawing with Harley about the goings-on over at The Pirate's Den. Lance had a good, reliable memory and he stored all these stories in his head.

"Go ahead, I'm waitin'."

Georgie twitched the ends of his burly mustache that rose like a devil's horns on either side of his mouth. Rose looked at him impatiently, then she downed her drink in one gulp and slammed the glass down on the bar. "All right, Georgie. I'll get back to work. If you want to tell the marshal anything in private, here's your chance."

She again ran a quick, nervous hand over Lance's billowing locks and gave him a come-hither look. "I'll see you later. When you don't have so much on your mind."

Having said that, Rose went back to the table where the tall, bearded cowboy at first ignored her. Then Rose whispered something in his ear and he laughed and pounded the table before shoving a chair out for her with one of his booted feet. Rose sat down.

The cowboy called for drinks and Georgie said, "I'll be right back, Marshal."

Lance fought his impatience. He had a murder on his hands and here he was letting business go on as usual. He would have closed down the Cutlass Room right then and there if he thought he would be within the law. Trouble was, he was just too green as a lawman to know what legal act he should take. He felt that he would just go along with the bartender until he got the name he was after. Then he would do some checking up. He had Gil in the back guarding Kidd's office so he had no worries on that score.

Georgie filled two glasses and took them over to the table where Rose was seated. He took his time while the cowboy paid him and finally came back to the bar.

"I'm waiting," Lance said.

"It was Mundy. Reuben Mundy was in here earlier. He and the Captain got into a real shoutin' match. The Captain had to finally throw him out."

"What was all the yellin' about?"

"Same thing Mundy always jaws about. How the Captain was a lowdown, cheatin' pig. Whenever Mundy got a snoot full, he always came back to the same old story. How he lost everything, ranch, cattle, horses. All because of what Martin Kidd done."

Lance didn't say anything but he was listening to every word Georgie was saying. It seemed to be the truth but the barkeep had exaggerated in the past. Quite possibly he was doing the same now. When he stopped talking Lance said, "Did Mundy say anything else?"

"Yep. He threatened to kill the Captain. That was when Kidd had him thrown out."

"When did all this happen?"

Georgie pulled thoughtfully on his mustache.

"Two, maybe three hours ago. You think maybe Munday had something to do with the killin'?"

Lance didn't give Georgie that satisfaction. "Might have, might not have. I'm going to check on my deputy."

"If you ask me, whoever done it deserves a medal."

"You didn't like Kidd?"

"He treated his help like dirt."

Lance gave Georgie a little extra consideration. The list of suspects was beginning to grow.

"Marshal? Business as usual here?"

Lance glanced around. "For the time being," he said and walked out of the room. In the hallway he looked carefully at everything as he walked toward Martin Kidd's office. But the hallway was clean, nothing to help him here.

Gil was still standing in the hallway.

"Grab a chair and sit down," Lance commanded. "No sense you standin' all the time. I gotta go check on Reuben Mundy."

"Mundy, he got something to do with this?"

"The barkeep, Georgie, heard him and Kidd have an argument. Mundy threatened to kill him."

Gil pulled up a chair and sank down in it stretching out his long, denim-clad legs.

"That's nothin' new. Mundy's been sayin' that for

months. I even heard him say it when I was down at the bowlin' alley one day."

"I know. Only this time he said it right before the Captain got his head bashed in. Kinda bad timing on Mundy's part."

Gil slowly nodded. "Guess it sounds that way. You goin' to arrest him?"

"Don't know. But I gotta find out where he was after he was thrown out of the bar."

"Kidd had him thrown out?"

"So I was told."

"Now where does Mundy live?"

Lance removed his Stetson and smoothed his dark head of hair, then put the hat back in place. "Got an idea. West of town, Harley said. Only house back in that part of town."

"If you want to call it a house. You can't miss it. A shame really."

"What is?"

"Oh, I knew Mundy when he had one of the biggest spreads in the county. That was before he lost it to Kidd."

"What's become of the land?"

Gil crossed his long, muscular legs. "Just gone back to nature. Don't know why Kidd held on to it. Hear rumors that it was where Hap Briley and his gang of thugs hang out. Probably true."

That was something Lance felt was worthwhile knowing. He hadn't thought about where Briley might hunker down.

"Better be headin' out to Mundy's place. You be all right here?"

Gil's head bobbed up and down. He was obviously enjoying playing the part of a deputy. "Don't concern yourself about me, Lance. I'll be fine. Nobody'll get past me while you're gone."

Gil pulled out a harmonica he carried in his vest pocket and slapped it against the palm of one hand before he raised it to his mouth.

Lance departed as the strains of "The Dreary Black Hills" played slightly off-key echoing down the silent hallway.

He went through the Cutlass Room for one last time and Georgie gave him a quick nod while Rose glanced at him with a look in her eyes that bothered Lance. Something wasn't quite right here. He didn't know what it was. Whether it was the atmosphere at The Den, Georgie's attitude, or whatever was different about Rose Sparks, he didn't know. It just made him watchful and uneasy.

As he went through the lobby, he saw that Cal Gordon was busy registering some folks at the desk. Even though the owner of the establishment was deceased, the people still came and signed the register, not knowing of the murder that had taken place beyond the Cutlass Room. He wondered what their reaction would be if they knew the body of Martin Kidd lay battered on the floor of his office.

Outside, Lance lifted himself into the saddle and urged the gelding away from the hotel.

He headed down the street and as he passed Denker's Mercantile, Harley came out. He held up a hand and Lance reined his horse to a stop.

"What's this I hear about the Captain? He a goner like I been told, Lance?"

Lance confirmed the rumor. "Looks like a burglary that got interrupted."

Harley chewed on his lower lip. "Sorry end to that man's life. Can't say I'm grievin' any over the loss. Got any idea who might've done it?"

"One or two. Right now I'm on my way over to Reuben Mundy's place. Want to jaw with him."

"Reuben Mundy! You speakin' the gospel truth?"

"The bartender over at The Den overheard a real lung contest between the Captain and Mundy. Georgie said Mundy even threatened to kill him."

Harley made a face. "Mundy's been doin' that for a long time. Just letting out air. He don't mean half the things he says about Martin Kidd."

"Maybe so. Anyway, I gotta find out where he was after he left The Den."

Harley chuckled.

"What's funny?"

"Not really funny. Just thinkin' we elected you marshal and already you're starting to clean up Jubilee."

"Looks that way. See you real soon, Harley," Lance said, as he moved away from the store. He couldn't put away the words Harley had said. No sooner had Crawley been taken away that things began to happen to Lance. Things beyond his control. He wasn't all that certain he liked the direction his life was taking.

Outside of town he stopped thinking of Harley Denker and what he had said. He was the marshal of Jubilee now and he better start acting like one.

Lance went into the countryside. It was lighted by the bright overhead sun. There was a faint breeze that carried with it the scent of sage and other spicy scents. Faraway stood the purple-hued mountains that looked like slumbering giants taking a lazy afternoon siesta.

The only thing that marred the beauty of the landscape was the Mundy place. It was a rambling, windburned shack with a make-shift corral. There was a mangy, unkempt pinto snorting inside the corral. Two dirty, unkempt kids were playing in the yard but they stopped when they saw Lance and ran inside the house.

Lance got off his gelding and tied the reins to a scrubby brush. When he looked up, a young boy was standing in the doorway. He was a mirror image of Reuben Mundy, so he had to be Mundy's son.

"Afternoon, Marshal," the boy said politely. He might have looked like Reuben, but that was as close a resemblance that he bore to his father. He was polite and respectful. Lance later assessed this was due to the ministrations of his mother. "I'm Daniel."

"Afternoon, Daniel," Lance said moving closer. "Wonder if I might ask you a question, Son."

"Anything I can help you with," Daniel said, and

moved aside as Reuben's wife Rachel stepped to the doorway. She was still a pretty woman, although living under the present conditions had taken their toll.

"Marshal," Rachel said. "I'm Reuben's wife. You may call me Rachel. Just what brings you out here?"

Lance got right to the point. "Your husband had an argument with Martin Kidd earlier today. I just wanted to have a word with him."

"Reuben sometimes speaks out of turn," Rachel said.

"Is that why Mr. Kidd sent you? Because Reuben and him had words?"

"No, Ma'am," Lance said. "Martin Kidd was killed not long after your husband threatened him."

The words came as a surprise to Rachel Mundy. You could tell by the gathering around her mouth and the look in her eyes. "Can't say I'm sorry, even though I don't wish no harm on anyone."

"Pa couldn't have done it," Daniel said, and Lance switched his attention to Reuben's eldest son.

"Why do you say that? And I wasn't accusin' your pa of anything . . . yet."

Daniel looked to his mother for guidance and she managed to let him know it was all right to speak without her speaking a word.

"Pa was home, here in bed. He's got a bad leg from the fall he took."

"What fall you talkin' about?" Lance asked.

"On the way home from The Den. His horse got spooked by something, maybe a rattler. Anyway, he threw pa and I found him lyin' out yonder. I brought him home."

Lance cocked his head and studied Daniel. The boy looked like he was speaking the truth. Just the same, Lance had a few questions to be answered.

"How long ago was that?"

Rachel spoke up. "Good four hours ago, Marshal. He's inside right now, in bed. You care to look?"

Lance had to know. So Rachel took him inside where Reuben Mundy lay sprawled on an old but clean blanket on his bed. It didn't take Saw Hogan to tell Lance that he was suffering and in a lot of pain. Rachel had wrapped his leg in a white bandage and it lay exposed outside the blanket. Lance thanked Rachel and went back outside.

"Pa was here for what Ma said, Marshal," Daniel said.

"I believe your ma," Lance said. "You take care of your pa and ma."

"Sure thing, Marshal," Daniel said, and a smile cut across his somber face. He became the young boy he was supposed to be with the smile. Lance tipped his Stetson and rode back to town.

He had to check off Reuben Mundy as a suspect. He thought the murder of Martin Kidd would be solved quickly. Mundy had made death threats, Mundy had made no bones about hating the very ground Kidd's boots trod. It had seemed too easy. It had been. Now Lance would have to look at other people, find out who hated the Captain enough to kill him. That wouldn't be as easy as it sounded. Lance hadn't met anyone who was overly fond of the departed.

At The Den, Lance tethered his horse to the hitchrail and walked quickly inside. He went through the bat-winged doors of the Cutlass Room and past the bar.

Georgie was cleaning the long mirror behind the bar, but Lance felt his eyes on him as he passed by.

When he got to the office of Martin Kidd, Gil was still sitting in the chair with his legs crossed and his Stetson pulled down over his eyes. He quickly got to his feet when Lance walked into the room.

"Saw Hogan ain't been here yet, I see," Lance said, looking at the still form of Martin Kidd on the floor.

"That drover you sent for him came back and said Hogan would be along any minute. Anything on Mundy?"

Lance shook his head. "He was in an accident. Horse threw him. Been in bed long before Kidd was murdered."

Gil stood with his hands thrust into his hip pockets. "Thought we had someone there."

"So did I. Now we gotta find out who else had it in for the Captain."

Gil made a noise from deep down inside his throat. "That won't be easy, half the town wanted him dead. The other half just wanted him out of Jubilee."

Lance had other thoughts in his head than Kidd's death. He was still anxious about Hap Briley and Uncle Ephraim's piebold. Somehow all that had gotten off-trail since the killing of the proprietor of The Den.

At that moment, Cal Gordon stuck his head around the corner of the open doorway.

"What's goin' on?" he asked.

Lance reached for him. "I got some questions for you," he said, pulling Cal inside.

Chapter Eleven

Once inside the office, Cal Gordon didn't struggle to free himself from Lance's tight grip.

"So it is true. The Captain's dead. I just came back to see for myself," Cal said.

Lance released his hold on the man.

"How did it happen? Who did him in?"

"Those were some of the questions I was about to ask you. Have you heard anything up at the desk that might help us?"

"All I heard was that he had been killed. The drover that went to fetch Hogan told me. That's all I know about all this."

Lance was disappointed. He felt that he wasn't getting anywhere with this murder. Maybe it was a mistake on his part accepting this job. Only he wasn't the type to give up easily. Otherwise he would still be in

San Anselmo and might never have heard of Jubilee and what had become of Uncle Ephraim.

"Sorry I pulled you in like that. Guess I'm just plain puzzled by all this. Got a lot on my mind lately. Not only Kidd's murder, but I lost track of somebody I was trying to find.

"Who's that?"

"Hap Briley. You ain't seen him have you?"

"Sure have. Right now he's asleep in the room off from the desk. He sometimes sleeps there whenever he's had a gutful of corn liquor or just plain tired."

Lance felt good again. Maybe things were getting turned around for him. Not only did he find the thief who stole Uncle Ephraim's horse, but maybe a person who might know something about the Captain's murder.

"This Briley wasn't all that loyal to Kidd, am I right?" Lance asked, somewhat anxious to go and wake up the sleeping hombre.

"He didn't like the Captain if that's what you mean. Matter of fact, Briley had told me more than once he'd like to put a bullet in the Captain."

"Briley say that lately?"

"Just the other day. Didn't like takin' orders, even from someone like Martin Kidd. Briley had grand ideas like takin' over the hotel for himself."

Gil scratched the back of his neck. "Got a good reason there for sending Kidd off on an early ride. Briley wanted the whole kit and kaboodle for himself."

"Sounds that way to me too," Lance said. "Where is this room where Briley's sleepin'? Would you take me there, Cal?"

"Any time you say, Marshal. He ain't goin' no place real soon. When I left the desk, he was sleepin' like a hibernatin' grizzly."

"Be right back, Gil."

"Maybe you want me to come along, Lance? Nobody's going to bother Martin Kidd."

"Better stay here, Gil. I can handle Hap Briley by myself."

Reluctantly, Gil nodded. He was getting anxious too, anxious for a little action. He didn't mind staying here with Kidd's dead body, that didn't bother him none. It was just that all those years of longing, all those years of waiting and hoping to be a lawman, didn't mean to turn out like this. But, he reckoned, being a lawman also meant you had to obey the man in command. In this case that man was Marshal Lance Jordan.

"If you need me, send Cal and I'll come a blastin'," Gil said.

"Hope there won't be any need for that," Lance said. Then, before he left, he put his hand on Cal's shoulder. "Thanks for being here, Cal. Need someone I can rely on. Really do appreciate all you're doin'."

"Better get movin' before Briley wakes up and hightails it out of here."

"Let's go, Cal," Lance said.

They walked down the hallway and through the

Cutlass Room which was beginning to swell up with customers. Word of the Captain's death must have spread like a prairie wildfire through the town.

There was a quick silence as Lance and Cal walked toward the door leading to the foyer. As soon as they went through the batwinged doors, the silent voices spoke up in one loud chorus. All the layabouts and no-goods in Jubilee were having an informal wake for the late owner of the Den. There was no sorrow at his passing, just another excuse to get roaring drunk.

In the foyer leading to the lobby, Lance paused for a moment listening to the hubbub inside the Cutlass Room.

"Not a lot of grievin' goin' on in there," he said.

Cal listened carefully and a smile spread slowly across his lips.

"Martin Kidd didn't have any friends. A lot of people claimed they were, but they were either afraid of him or just plain liars."

"Even an hombre like Kidd needs to have his death checked into," Lance said bluntly.

"Even if he was such a cheatin' lowlife?"

"Even so."

Cal took a deep breath and looked back once again at the Cutlass Room.

"Folks in there wouldn't agree with you, Marshal."

"Maybe not. Only thing I can say to that is the law is for everyone in Jubilee or it ain't much of a law."

"Reckon you're right," Cal said thoughtfully.

"Reckon we got ourselves a real marshal for a change."

Lance didn't answer to that, instead he said, "Where's this place that I can find Briley?"

"I'll take you there. Just come along with me," Cal said, and the two men walked out of the foyer and across the lobby to the front desk.

It was quiet this time of day, all you could hear was the men in the Cutlass Room airing their lungs. Off from the area where Cal worked was a small room. In it was a cot and some blankets. It was only a few feet wide, but there was a tiny end table near the bed and there was a window above the cot for airing out the otherwise smelly room.

"He's inside there," Cal said, pointing beyond the counter. "Looks like he's still pounding the pillow."

Lance walked past the counter and touched the half-opened door with his hand and it swung full wide. The sleeping man on the cot became instantly aware of the change and his eyes popped open. Hap Briley took one look at Lance and he was wide awake. He quickly reached across the cot toward the small table nearby.

Lance was lightning quick when he saw that Briley was going for his six-shooter. He leaped across the room and landed on top of Briley, blocking his move for his gun.

The two men struggled on the narrow cot for a moment and then toppled over to the floor. Briley took a badly aimed swipe at Lance's shoulder, but it had no kick to it. Lance came back with a quick, powerful jab to Briley's jaw and he heard something crack inside. Blood gushed out of one side of Briley's mouth, but the hombre didn't seem to care or notice.

Drawing his leg up beneath Lance's body, he summoned what little strength he had left and managed to throw Lance off balance and he was flung back through the open doorway. By the time he got to his feet, Briley had slipped out of the open window and was gone.

"Where does that lead to?" Lance yelled at Cal when he got to his feet.

"The back of The Den. I think that's where Briley has his horse tied up."

"Uncle Ephraim's piebold," Lance murmured as he moved past Cal and out of the room.

"Who's Uncle Ephraim?" Cal yelled after Lance.

Lance just shook his head as he bolted for the front door. Once outside he leaped into the saddle and headed the gelding toward the back of the building. But he was too late. He arrived just as the piebold bearing Hap Briley disappeared in a swirl of dry dust around the corner of the building.

Lance spurred his horse who responded with a sudden gallop. They made the end of the alley in a split second and then headed for the open land where Lance could see the lone rider making quick tracks to get away from him as quickly as possible.

Overhead, the sun beat down on Lance and he could feel the hot, dry warmth on his shoulders and hands. The breeze, fanned up by the speed of his gelding, cooled his face, but the dry dust stung his eyes and caked the edges of his mouth.

Ahead of him, the distance was narrowing between himself and the fleeing gunfighter. Lance kept his eyes on Briley's back thinking that maybe he had the killer of Captain Martin Kidd. If not, then he would arrest Briley for being a horse thief. There would be no other explanation for his having the piebold. Uncle Ephraim would never have parted with the horse. He wouldn't even have gambled it away.

Unexpectedly, over his shoulder, Briley fired four quick shots at Lance. It came as such a surprise that Lance pulled hard on the reins and his gelding came to a sudden halt. Grabbing the saddle horn, Lance barely missed sprawling head first into a thicket of thorny brush.

It had been a mistake, a reflex he should have guarded against. Those few moments gave Briley an edge and he took it willingly.

Lance spurred his gelding once more in pursuit. He could see that Briley had headed in a different direction. The plume of dust marked his trail so there was no trouble in following.

It all looked so familiar to Lance now that he had a chance to get his bearings. Yes, he reckoned, this was the way he had come when he had ridden out to the Abbott's place. To his right stood the stand of trees where he had been bushwacked—where he had found the traces of blood—Hap Briley's blood. He must have seen Saw Hogan and had the wound tended to.

The wound must not have been too bad. Briley rode the saddle straight as a broom handle.

Briley was headed right for the Abbott place. Lance felt sure Briley hadn't planned it that way. He had just taken the path by chance, now he was headed for the ranch where Harriett and Tom lived. Today was a holiday for the school and so Harriett would be home. That thought popped into Lance's head as he tried to gain back the distance between himself and the gunslinger—the distance he had lost when Briley had taken the shots at him.

Uncle Ephraim's piebold was a good runner, faster than Lance's gelding. Back in San Anselmo, Lance had raced his uncle many times but had eaten the dust laid out by the piebold. Then he remembered how his uncle had gloated over the victory. Too much so, taking every opportunity he could find to make Lance look like a born loser. Funny, Lance thought, how he recalled these things. He couldn't dredge up any good memories of his uncle. Lance supposed that was because there weren't all that many. But as bad a person as Uncle Ephraim was, he didn't deserve to be killed in a place called Jubilee, so far from his home in New Mexico.

Urging his gelding on, Lance did his best to try and catch up with Briley. By this time, he was certain Briley had arrived at the Abbotts.

In a few minutes, Lance drew hard on the reins bringing his horse to a quick standstill. Ahead of him stood the Abbott ranch house. The piebold stood be-

fore the open door and it didn't take much for Lance
to figure out where Briley had disappeared to.

Lance jumped down from his saddle and his right
hand went for his Colt .45. He was in a crouching
position as he went toward the house. He listened in-
tently, but there was nothing to hear save for the soft
sighting of a western breeze that moaned around the
eaves of the house and whispered in the sagebrush that
stood guard near the ranch on the desert.

Then abruptly, he heard voices and out of the house
came two figures. One was Harriett Abbott and behind
her, with a six-shooter pressed against her temple, was
Hap Briley.

Lance froze, not expecting anything like this to happen. He later remembered the cool, calm look in Harriett's eyes, but there was also an angry set to her
mouth. She didn't like what was happening to her
against her will and it showed.

Once outside the open door of the house, Briley
shouted, "Drop the gun, Jordan. If you don't want anything to happen to this woman, you'll do as I say."

Lance was tempted to do what Briley said but instead he kept the Colt level on Briley and Harriett.

"This won't get you any place, Briley. Why did you
draw on me back there at The Den? And why did you
run away?"

"You didn't come to see me on a social call," Briley
answered. "When I saw you in the doorway, I knew
it meant nothing but trouble."

Taking a chance Lance said, "Did you kill Martin Kidd?"

Briley was genuinely surprised at what Lance had said. It showed in his face.

Then Briley threw back his head and roared with laughter. "Kidd is dead? Now ain't that a hellava thing! Somebody finally laid him out!"

Lance stood his ground and waited until Briley had finished laughing. Harriett was looking straight ahead, as though she hadn't heard a word from Lance or Briley's near-maniacal laugh.

"I'm waitin' for an answer," Lance repeated in a cool, low-pitched voice.

"I wish it hadda been me. I hated that bastard's guts."

"Enough to kill him?"

"Sure. But I didn't. Which don't mean I haven't done my share of killing at The Den. Last I saw of him was yesterday. If I'd known he was goin' downstairs, I would have bought him a drink to send him on his way."

Lance was getting anxious now. He had to control himself, watch what he was saying. He had Harriett to think about. He wouldn't put it past Briley to carry out his threat to kill Harriett. Lance had heard rumors around town that Briley had done in a party girl down in Bisbee a few years back. So killing a woman wasn't beyond him.

"Where'd you latch on to that piebold?" Lance

changed the subject quickly. He wanted answers to other questions too.

"It was a gift," Briley said with a quick chuckle. "A gift from the dearly departed. Fella what rode into Jubilee on it doesn't need it any more."

As steady as he could manage, Lance said, "You mean the man who rode it was killed, don't you."

"Right, Mr. Marshal. Done in by the Captain. Wasn't the first one, I might add."

At that moment, Harriett gave Lance a signal. A signal not with words but something in her eyes that was quick as a prairie fox. He knew she was going to do something and he tightened his grip on the Colt.

Harriett suddenly moaned and sank into a heap at the feet of the gunslinger. It caught Briley by surprise and his grip on her loosened as she sagged to the ground. At that moment Lance yelled out, "Drop it, Briley!"

But Briley wasn't to be taken in. His arm jerked as he raised his gun to get off a few rounds. He wasn't quick enough. Lance's gun spat flame and a curl of smoke. The bullets struck Briley with such an impact, he seemed to dance a fast step or two as his shirt front burst open and blood gushed in a quick pattern across his chest.

Briley sank to the ground still clutching his six-shooter. Lance rushed over to help Harriett to her feet. They both looked down at Briley who lay on his side, his mouth twisted and agape and his eyes wide with disbelief.

"Is he dead?" Harriett whispered in a voice raw with choked emotion.

Lance squatted and touched Briley's throat. There was no pulse. He looked up at Harriett and nodded.

Harriett broke down now that the danger had passed. She sobbed quietly into a kerchief she carried in the pocket of her dress. Lance would have comforted her, but he felt it was best to let her cry this out.

Harriett didn't cry long. This was something she had almost grown used to here in the unrelenting western code of living. *This would never do*, she thought, *I'm not helping Lance out one bit by crying*. She wiped her damp cheeks and said, "You did what you had to do, Lance. There was no other way. He was an evil man."

"At least I found out he didn't kill Martin Kidd."

"I heard about that. Even out here we have our telegraph system. Was Mr. Briley a suspect?"

"One of them. I seem to take one step forward for every two I step backwards."

Lance seemed somewhat discouraged. Harriett touched him on the arm. "You'll find who did it, Lance. You are a bright young man."

"Thanks, Harriett. I'll do what I can. At least now I know what became of my uncle's horse and who killed him."

Lance didn't think he should stay much longer at the Abbotts. "Will you be all right? I should take Briley's body into town. Saw Hogan will have a little business with him."

"I'll be fine. You just do what you have to do, Lance."

Lance reached down and picked up Briley's body. He carried the slain man to Uncle Ephraim's horse and steadied the skittish piebold, while he anchored Briley across the saddle.

He made sure that Harriett was all right before he eased himself into his own saddle.

"Tom should be along at any time," Harriett said. "I'll be just fine. Don't you worry none."

With one backward glance, he headed back to Jubilee with the body of Hap Briley.

Lance now had two suspects that had proven to not be the guilty party. Mundy was home nursing a broken leg and Briley was taking his last ride on the piebold. So where was he as far as finding out who killed the Captain? Nothing was cut and dry in this life. Lance had always been aware of that, but now the truth of it hit him like a galloping herd of buffalo.

Beyond the stand of trees, Lance saw a rider headed in his direction. The nearer the rider approached, the more Lance became convinced it was Tom Abbott. By the time the bay pinto got close to a wild spitting distance, Tom reined in the horse.

"Yo, Lance, what's going on? Who you got on the piebold?"

Tom waited until Lance drew alongside him. Then Tom saw for himself. "Hap Briley! He's a goner?"

"Had to shoot it out with him. Taking him back to town to see Saw Hogan."

"What happened?"

Carefully, so as not to get Tom unnecessarily riled up, Lance told him about the fight in The Den. How he had chased Briley to Tom's ranch. When he got to the part where Harriett was held at gunpoint, Tom's face turned snake-belly white and he jerked his head to look in the direction of the ranch.

"Don't worry, Harriett's fine. Briley didn't get a chance to harm her."

"I gotta go, Lance. I want to see Harriett. You understand?"

"Right, I understand. I'd do the same thing if I was in your boots."

Tom just tipped his hat and spurred the pinto and rode into the wind toward the ranch.

It was now only a short ride to Jubilee. Lance urged his gelding on, aware of how skittish the animal was with the piebold carrying its burdensome load.

When Lance reached the outskirts of Main Street, he headed not for The Den, but Saw Hogan's office. He figured by this time Hogan should have Kidd's body at the mortuary. He was right. Hogan met him at the door. Smiling.

"I think we'd better have a little talk," Lance said after he helped carry Briley's body inside. "About what's been goin' on here between you and the Captain. You understand what I'm sayin'?"

Hogan had been drinking, but not heavily. His

speech was clear, even though his eyes were somewhat puffy and bloodshot.

"How much you know?"

Lance told him, most of it the exact words he had
heard, and some of it speculation. Each word seemed
to pierce Hogan like an arrow.

"It's true. It didn't start out that way. At first I just
went along with a couple of men who were just single
with no living relatives. What difference did it make,
I thought. Nobody would miss them. Then I got in
deeper. Kidd made me. He told me I had to keep at it
or he would expose me and I'd end up in the Yuma
prison."

Lance listened without much pity. Hogan was a
weak man and one who would blame others for his
own shortcomings.

"Telling me all this won't help your chances when
it comes to the judge comin' in from Tucson on the
stage."

"You planning on locking me up?"

"You broke the law."

Saw Hogan seemed to crumble before Lance's eyes.
He was a broken man. A man who almost welcomed
having his past behavior found out.

"That being the case, I'd better tell you that Martin
Kidd didn't die from those blows to his head."

Lance couldn't help but show his surprise at what
Hogan said. "What are you tellin' me?"

"I'm telling you Martin Kidd died from a stab
wound. Right to the heart."

"But he was hit on the head by that poker."

"Don't disagree with that."

"Then whoever done it hit the Captain to hide the real cause of his death."

"Appears that way."

Something he had seen, or hadn't seen, bothered Lance when he heard what Saw Hogan had said. All day, since he had found the body of Martin Kidd, and even before, he had been bothered by it. Then he remembered. It was like waking up after a bad dream and finding bits and pieces of the dream still with you.

At that moment, Gil barged into the room. He pushed his Stetson to the back of his head which had become a habit with him.

"Thought that was your gelding out there. Cal told me you were after Briley." Gill looked at the still form of Hap Briley on the table. "Looks like you found him."

"He drew on me. It was a fair fight."

"Just wanted to tell you that Cal told me Briley couldn't have killed the Captain. He was asleep when it happened."

"I know," Lance said. "I've got a pretty sure idea who done it. You stick around here. Keep an eye on Hogan. I don't want him takin' any sudden rides anywhere."

Gil nodded. "Sure will. Where you headed?"

"Back to The Den. I'm goin' to clear all this up once and for all."

* * *

Lance rode the short distance to The Pirate's Den and walked briskly through the lobby to the Cutlass Room. The layabouts and free-loaders had emptied out somewhat. A few die-hards were holding up the mahogany bar.

Lance went directly to Georgie who was cleaning a glass with a dish towel. When Lance approached, he put the glass and the wiper aside, his hands rested beneath the rim of the bar.

"Where's Rose?" Lance demanded in a hard voice.

"Ain't seen her," Georgie said, but Lance could tell he was lying. "Anyway, what you want her for?"

"None of your business," Lance said watching Georgie's every move. "Now, where is she?"

Georgie took that moment to reach for his shotgun, but Lance was faster. He drew his Colt and reached out and snatched the shotgun from Georgie's hands. "Now! Where is Rose!"

Georgie swallowed hard, sweat beaded his forehead. "She's in her place. Back of The Den."

"Thanks," Lance said. "I'll keep this for now."

He left the Cutlass Room by the back entrance where he passed the Captain's office. Pausing at the room, he slid the shotgun across the floor where it was hidden beneath the desk. Then he went out the back door.

Rose's small house was just a few feet from The Den. Lance walked over and pounded on the front door which was bolted.

In a few seconds Rose called out, "Who's there?"

"Marshal Jordan," Lance said, but it still sounded funny his calling himself marshal.

"Hold your longjohns on," Rose replied, and in a few moments opened the door.

"Business or pleasure?" Rose said in a voice that was not interested in either at the moment.

"I need to talk to you, Rose," Lance said.

Rose stood aside. "Come on in. I never say no to any law enforcer."

It was a surprisingly feminine and cozy room with all sorts of frills you wouldn't expect from Rose Sparks of the many towns and many faces.

"You missin' something, Rose? I noticed earlier you looked different."

Immediately Rose's hands went to her hair. She caught herself in mid-air, then she sighed and put one hand on one ample hip. "You noticed it, huh?"

"I noticed. Where is it, Rose? Where's the comb you used to stab Martin Kidd with? You did kill him, didn't you?"

Rose didn't blink an eye. She wasn't the type of person who would beg for mercy or cry to get any sympathy. Instead she walked over to the bed and drew back the mattress. She picked up the hair comb and handed it to Lance. The blade had been wiped off but there were still specks of brown-dried blood stains on it and the handle.

"Why did you do it, Rose?" Lance asked, putting the knife in his vest pocket.

"I told him, I told that bastard, if he ever hit me

again it would be the last time. No man does that to me. My old man did when I was a kid, but I swore I wouldn't let no man do that when I was big enough to look after Rose."

Then she told him how Martin had been in his office and she had walked in. He had said words to her and then slapped her across the face. Rose said she just grabbed the knife and stuck him. Then she picked up the poker and hit him to make it look like a burglar had done it.

"The knife made such a small hole in his chest. I didn't think anyone would notice. Then I messed up the office and took my knife to my room."

Lance looked around the room and then said, "Better not say any more, Rose."

"Yeah," Rose said, and her mouth twisted into a mocking grin. "I can tell it to the hangman, right?"

Chapter Twelve

"When will you be back?" Gil asked, as Lance finished strapping the saddlebag to his gelding.

"Soon as I can," Lance said. "Soon as Susan and me get married. You think you can handle things until I get back?"

Gil wasn't sure, but he didn't want Lance to worry none. After all, he was going to get hitched up, that would be enough for him to worry about.

Tom and Harriett had come by earlier that morning. Harriett had prepared some food for the trip back to San Anselmo. They were both a little saddened that Lance was leaving, but he assured them he would be coming back.

"Susan will want to come back with me," he assured them. "You'll take to her like I know she'll take to you."

"We'll hold you to your word," Tom said. Then he shook hands with Lance and Harriett gave him a quick, light hug. "Take care," she said.

Lance earlier had walked down to see Harley Denker before he left. The old man gave him a pat on the back and said, "Remember, your old job is always here if you decide law abidin' work ain't for you. And another thing, you can get as much free lumber as you need to build your nest."

"No way to run a business," Lance said and grinned.

"It's my business, I can run it any way I dern please."

So that had been earlier this day and now Lance was ready to ride out of Jubilee and make tracks back to San Anselmo. Strapped securely to his saddle was the money, all of it, that Uncle Ephraim had taken. Cal Gordon had found it in the safe untouched by Rose Sparks.

Rose and Saw Hogan had been in opposite cells while they waited trial. It had been swift and certain when the judge from Tucson had come to town.

A lot of men had been at the stage line when Rose had boarded it under guard. It had been a high moment for her. She had become something of a legend in the county for her dispatching Captain Martin Kidd.

When the stage pulled out for its final destination, Rose waved at the men with a blood-red kerchief and you could hear her laughter over the noise of the galloping horses.

"Things should be quieting down here in Jubilee, now," Lance had said to Gil.

"The Pirate's Den is shutting its doors. Too bad, but nobody wants to take a chance in buying the place."

"Maybe that's just as well," Lance had told Gil as he began getting ready to leave Jubilee.

"End of an era," Reuben Mundy had said, leaning heavily on a crutch fashioned out of an old oak limb.

"Can't say I'm especially sad the Captain's gone or his kingdom either."

"The town might get respectable now," Lance replied. "With a little help from the townsfolk."

Over the next rise, beyond the dry wash, he would find Susan. If she was away for the time being Lance would wait. But he knew Susan would be there, something deep within told him to hurry.

He spurred the gelding and the setting sun blazed like a brilliant star in the west, welcoming him home.